DNA

Doesn't Lie

DNA Doesn't Lie

Published in the United States of America
ISBN Paperback: 978-1-960629-49-4
ISBN eBook: 978-1-960629-50-0

ReadersMagnet, LLC
10620 Treena Street, Suite 230 | San Diego, California, 92131 USA
1.619. 354. 2643 | www.readersmagnet.com

Cover design by Kent Gabutin
Interior design by Daniel Lopez

DNA
Doesn't Lie

CHERI LEPAGE

ReadersMagnet, LLC

DEDICATION

This book is dedicated to my husband, Dan, who is my soul mate and the inspiration for my story. To my daughters, Sandra and Megan, who have fulfilled my dream of being a mother, and to Brooklyn, my granddaughter who is a great artist.

PROLOGUE

1990

When Chris Regan saw Elena Sparkman for the first time at a company function, he'd been instantly attracted to her. Since she was there with Jacob, a coworker of his, Chris decided she wasn't meant for him.

Later that evening when they were introduced, he took hold of her hand to shake it, and as he did so, a strong sensation of love crept across his hand, up his arm, stopping at his heart. He was dazed by the occurrence as it was the strangest reaction to a woman he'd ever experienced before.

Thinking their touch had only affected *him*; he was stunned when she gave his hand a tight squeeze and winked at him. He wanted to ask her out right then and there, but it would have to wait until later, as he couldn't very well invite her out in front of her date.

Besides, he had to do something first. Since he wasn't the type of guy to date two women at the same time, before he could ask Elena out, he had to tell Olivia Reinhardt, a woman he'd been dating for the past two months, that it was over between them.

When he called Olivia and told her he wouldn't be seeing her any more, she began sobbing. He felt bad for hurting her, but their relationship just wasn't meant to be, as there wasn't any spark when he kissed her. Keeping the fact, he was interested in someone else to himself, he simply told her it was time for them to go their separate ways.

The next day at work, Chris asked for Elena's number from Beth, his coworker's assistant, and since Beth didn't want Elena in Jacob, her boss's life, she happily gave it to him. When he called Elena, he asked about Jacob first, as he didn't want to step on any toes. When he learned, Jacob was only a good friend; Chris took a deep breath and asked her out. When he hung up five minutes later, Chris let out a scream of excitement as he had a date with her for Friday night.

When it was time to go to pick Elena up, he picked up his car keys and started for the door, but before he could open it, the phone started ringing. He debated about answering, but thinking it could be Elena, he grabbed it.

But it wasn't Elena, but Olivia wanting him to give her another chance, but he stayed firm with his decision. Since there wasn't any reason to continue going out with a woman that didn't entice him sexually, he told her good-bye, hung up and started for the door again. This time when the phone rang, he simply opened the door and walked out of his apartment, closing it behind him, as the phone continued ringing.

***

When he arrived at Elena's apartment complex, he parked his car, and got out, but before he could reach the steps to her apartment, Elena came out to meet him.

"Hello," she called to him.

He smiled at her. "Are you so anxious to go out with me that you can't wait for me to knock on the door?" he teased.

She blushed at his joke. "Now, you know how I feel about you."

Chris hurried up the steps and pulled her into his arms.

Elena let out a squeal of surprise at his actions, but before she could say anything, he brought his lips to hers. The kiss was explosive; so much so, that he knew she was the woman for him.

His kiss was so breathtaking; Elena' knees gave out on her, and if it hadn't been for the fact Chris was holding her, she would have fallen.

"Now you know how I feel about you," he whispered in her ear.

"I've never been kissed like that before."

"If you marry me, I'd kiss you like that for the rest of our lives."

Elena leaned back to look him in the eyes. "Did you just propose to me?"

"It wasn't a very good proposal if you have to ask," he teased, giving her a happy grin.

"Chris, we haven't even gone out on our first date yet."

"Why waste our time dating, when we can get married and start on our family right away."

Tears filled her eyes, as this was all too good to believe. "You want a baby right away?" As this was something, she'd been dreaming about since she was a young girl. Never dating a man that she wanted to marry, she gave up the thought that it would ever be a possibility. Now that it was, she was afraid to blink, thinking it could all disappear in a puff of smoke.

"Yes, as I can't wait to see you with our child growing inside your belly."

"Oh, Chris. I don't know what to say."

"It's either yes or no," he said with a teasing smile.

She hugged him around his neck. "Yes. My answer is yes, I'll marry you."

He gave her a passionate kiss to seal the deal. "Is tomorrow too soon?" he asked breathlessly.

She laughed. "Can we at least have one date before we get married?"

He chuckled at her joke. "If you insist, but then we're getting married."

"Chris, can we have an appetizer before dinner?" she asked seriously.

He gave her a puzzled look. "Well, sure. What did you have in mind?" he asked. He was expecting her to tell him the usual kinds of appetizer, like mozzarella sticks, fried mushroom, etc., but instead, she put her hand on his arousal, causing him to jump.

"I want you to be the appetizer."

Chris couldn't take a chance she may change her mind, so he grabbed hold of her hand and started them toward the door to her apartment complex. "Then we better get started."

***

They went to dinner at a dark romantic restaurant, one where it felt as if they were the only two people in the place. Unbeknown to Chris and Elena, they were enjoying their first and last meal together as a couple.

Marilyn, Olivia's best friend was sitting at the next table with her husband, so when she saw Chris with another woman, she picked up her cell phone and quickly dialed Olivia's number.

"Hello?"

"Olivia, this is Marilyn."

"You sound strange. Is something wrong?"

"I'm at Ginni's Restaurant and Chris is here with an attractive blond. They must be on a date because they're feeding each of bits of food from their plates, looking dreamy into each other's eyes. I just wanted you to know he's cheating on you."

"I appreciate you calling, but he broke up with me two nights ago. He's the only man I've ever wanted," she cried to her friend. The truth was she wanted him because he was the only man to dump her, as she usually did the breaking up.

"How come you didn't tell me the two of you broke up," she said, hurt her friend hadn't told her.

"I was hoping he would come back to me before I had to tell you. I've been calling his home every few minutes, but since he hadn't answer, I assumed that he was simply not answering the phone."

"What are you going to do about getting him back?"

An evil grin filled her face, as she knew that Chris had to pay for discarding her for another woman. "I'm going to blackmail him into coming back to me.

"Blackmail?" Marilyn asked, instantly regretting making this call to her friend. What she didn't understand was why anyone would want a man that definitely didn't want you, but she kept her opinion to herself. She knew that Olivia could be malicious when someone did or said something she didn't like, so she hated to think what she was going to do to Chris.

"Once I confront him, he won't have a choice but to come back into my life," she said, letting out an evil giggle. "Do you know who the woman is?"

"I heard Chris call her Elena, but I didn't I hear a last name." Even if she had known the woman's last name, she wouldn't have given it to her.

"Damn! I have to know who she is. I'll have to hire a private investigator and he can find out who she is. I'll probably have to keep him on retainer, so I'll know if Chris cheats on me after we're married."

"Well good luck with that," she said, hoping her friend didn't notice her sarcastic tone.

"I'll call you when I start planning the wedding."

"You do that," Marilyn said then disconnected the phone call. She felt guilty for calling her, as she was sure Olivia was going to make Chris' life hell because of her call, and he didn't deserve that.

***

After their evening out, Chris brought Elena home and ended up spending the night in her bed, and during one of the many times they made love, their child was conceived.

The next morning, he kissed her good-bye and told her he'd call her later. Once outside, he got into his car and drove to back to his apartment, singing along with the radio, not even dreaming that his world was about to drop to the lowest level of Hell.

***

Olivia worked her evil magic and when she had everything in place, she went to Chris' apartment to tell him what she wanted from him. Once there, she moistened her lips and pinched her cheeks, then she knocked at the door.

When Chris opened the door, he was smiling, as he was expecting Elena to arrive any moment. When he saw it was Olivia standing there, his smile disappeared, and he just stood there staring at her.

"Aren't you happy to see me?" she asked coyly.

"What do you what?" he asked nervously, as he was afraid Elena would show up before Olivia left.

"Aren't you going to ask me in?"

"No."

"I'm sure your neighbors will just love hearing about our dirty laundry."

"What dirty laundry would that be?" he asked. As his eyes studied her, he realized that she was up to something, but he couldn't figure out what it could be.

"About me having your baby," she said smoothly as if it was the truth, which they both knew it wasn't. "Now are you going to ask me in?"

Chris could only stare at her is bewilderment. "You can't be pregnant with my child as we haven't ever had sex," he said loud enough for any of his neighbors who might be listening to hear.

She gave him a smile that told him she wanted something from him. "Let me in and we'll talk about it," she uttered in a lowered voice.

"Just spit it out Olivia and tell me what it is you want."

Since he wouldn't let her into his apartment, she figured that Elena was in there with him and the thought made her angry. "I want to be your wife," she said quietly.

Chris laughed. "Not in this life time, sugar."

She leaned closer to him. "My father is on the Board of Directors of the bank that holds your grandfather's mortgage. Daddy will believe whatever I tell him, so if you don't want him to think that you knocked me up and then refused to marry me, I suggest you change your mind."

His eyes grew round as he didn't doubt, she would do exactly what she threatened if she didn't get her way. And knowing her father, Chris was certain he would foreclose on his grandfather's loan in a split second if he thought he'd gotten his precious angel knocked up. Damn, he was in a pickle.

"That's blackmail." His grandfather had refinanced his mortgage on his land to help put Chris through college, since the new loan was only five years old that meant, Chris would have to stay married to Olivia for the next twenty-five years. What a horrible thought! But if he refused to marry Olivia, Mr. Reinhardt would make sure his grandfather couldn't find another bank anywhere on this planet to give him another loan.

"You call it whatever you want. Since I want you as my husband, I plan to do whatever's necessary to obtain you in my life."

"Why would you want to marry me when you know that I don't love you?"

She gave him a sly grin. "You're the man I want and I always get what I want."

"Go to hell." Chris slammed the door in her face, then instantly regretted his rash actions, as this conversation proved it wasn't smart to make Olivia Reinhardt angry. When he heard her chuckling outside his door, his hands tightened into fists, as he knew she had him over a barrel.

"I'll give you an hour, and if I don't hear from you by then, I'm going to my father. If you want to save your grandfather's place, I suggest you change your answer before then."

His grandfather had raised him after the death of his parents, Colin and Marjorie Regan. His grandfather had been both father and mother to him; he couldn't be the cause of him to lose the land that meant the world to him. He didn't want to let her win this game, but he couldn't let Albert Regan lose his home either, so that only left one choice and that was to give in to her blackmail and marry her.

"She may be able to force me to marry her, but she can wait until Hell freezes over before I'll ever love that bitch," he said softly to the empty room. But before he called Olivia, he had to talk to Elena explain why he couldn't marry her.

When Elena arrived, Chris explained about Olivia's blackmail. As she cried, he held her, telling her that he would try to find his grandfather other financing, but it might take time, something he didn't have much of just now.

Elena realized she would have to leave town, as she couldn't marry him and be the cause of his grandfather losing his home. So in order to make sure Chris married Olivia, she broke up with him, telling him she was going to go live with her parents in Ohio.

Chris tried to talk her out of leaving town, but she refused. She knew if she stayed in Kansas City, they would continue to be lovers, and she refused to be *other* woman.

***

After Elena left, he called Olivia to tell her he would marry her. When she let out a cackle that caused his skin to crawl, he realized he'd just sold his sole to the devil and wished that he and Elena had just eloped and hell with the consequence. Oh, how he regretted getting involved with such a cold-hearted woman in the first place.

Not trusting her to keep her word regarding his grandfather's loan, he told her that she would have to sign a document that stated the loan wouldn't be foreclosed on as long as they were married. Olivia laughed at his request, saying she wouldn't sign anything until their wedding day.

When Chris hung up the phone from Olivia, he drove out to his grandfather's ranch to tell him about the wedding. He knew he couldn't tell him they were in love, as his grandfather knew he loved another. He also couldn't tell him about the blackmail, so he simply told him that Elena had left him and this wedding to Olivia was just a business deal, which was in part was the truth.

Albert tried to talk him out of marrying a woman he knew he didn't love, but Chris wouldn't budge. Not wanting to be part of his grandson's horrible mistake, he refused to come to the farce of a wedding.

After Chris had called Olivia to tell her that he would marry her, she called her minister and set a time for wedding for the next Saturday. The sooner they were married, the sooner they would have sex, which meant the quicker she would be pregnant, tightening the loose around Chris' neck. After she hung up the phone, she just sat there with a smile on her face, as her blackmailing scheme had turned out to be easier than she thought.

When Olivia called Marilyn to invite her to the wedding, she gave her regrets, saying she had to work and wouldn't be able to make it. No way, no how was Marilyn going to stand there and watch Chris marry a woman he didn't love because of her.

***

When Chris arrived at the church for the wedding, he saw Fraser and Vanne Reinhardt were already there. When he didn't see any sign of Olivia, he hoped she'd changed her mind about marrying him, but seriously doubted he would be so lucky.

"Hello, Mr. and Mrs. Reinhardt."

"So you knocked up my daughter," Fraser taunted, giving Chris a nasty look.

"No, sir I'm not the father of your daughter's baby," Chris said, not caring what her parents thought of him.

"When a baby arrives and looks just like you, we'll know for sure now won't we?" Fraser replied spitefully.

"It isn't going to look like me because I haven't ever had sex with her. If she's really pregnant, the baby isn't mine," he muttered, as he refused to claim another man's child as his own.

His reply angered Fraser, as he knew his daughter wouldn't have lied to them about the father of her child. "I don't believe you."

"I don't care what you believe," he replied, looking the older man in the eye.

"Do you love our daughter?" Fraser asked, not at all prepared for Chris reply.

"No, I don't," he stated honestly, as he kept his eyes on Fraser.

Olivia's mother gasped.

"If you don't love her, then why are you marrying her?" Fraser asked, watching him closely as he waited for his response.

"Because she's blackmailing me, something I'm sure she learned from you."

Chris retort surprised Fraser, but it made him proud of Olivia to know she was just like a chip off the old block. "How can she blackmail you?"

"If I don't marry her, she'll have you foreclose on my grandfather's mortgage."

"And I would. I still believe you're lying about being the baby's father."

"I'm marrying her, so what more do you want from me?" he asked hatefully.

Before Fraser could reply, Olivia stepped into the room. Since it was going to be just her parents and the two of them for the wedding, the minister started the ceremony as soon as Olivia reached the front of the church.

Chris stopped the proceedings by interrupting the minister, as he had to be sure Olivia signed the document to protect his grandfather before they went any further, because once he said 'I do' she could refuse to sign it.

Once that was done and the document was in his pocket, the wedding begun. With each word of the service, Chris felt as if nail was being hammered into his heart, as he was tying himself to a woman he'd come to hate. As Chris looked around the room, he wasn't surprised that the bride was the only one who looked happy about this wedding taking place.

***

Olivia assumed she'd won the war, but soon learned it was only a battle she'd had achieved victory over that day. For as soon as they were pronounced husband and wife, without even kissing his bride or saying a farewell to her, Chris turned and walked out the door. The three left behind, hollered at him to return, but he kept on walking.

So disgusted at the fact that he'd married the wrong woman, he knew he had to get out of the church before he did something he'd come to regret, like strangling her. He'd given her what she wanted, what more did she want from him? When he reached his car, he got in, and drove off before they could follow him and stop him from leaving.

Just because he had been forced to marry Olivia, he refused to change his plans for her as he and a coworker were scheduled to fly out for a business meeting in New York. So instead of starting his honeymoon with his new wife, he drove to the airport without Olivia knowing where he was going or when he would be back.

When he'd made his flight arrangements, he'd scheduled a short lay over in Cincinnati in the hopes of seeing Elena. When he reached Cincinnati, he called

Elena to tell her he was in town and would like to see her.

"Chris, as much as I would love to see you, I can't be the other woman."

"I wish I hadn't married that bitch as she took the only woman I'll ever love away from me," he shouted angrily.

Elena sighed over the phone. "I couldn't marry you and be the cause of your grandfather losing his land."

"I know, but now you and I have lost everything, while Olivia's evil scheming has achieved what she wanted."

"Why did she want you, if she knew you didn't love her?"

"Because I had the nerve to break up with her, that's why."

"Thanks for flying up here to see me, but please go home to your wife."

"Elena, please don't do this to us," he said, as his tears fell down his cheeks.

"You're married now, so please don't call this number again or I'll have no other choice but to change it."

"Please don't do that. I promise not to call you, as I couldn't stand to know I couldn't get hold of you if I needed to."

"Okay, I won't do anything for now."

"Please call me if you ever change your mind or in need of something."

"I will."

Chris waited around the busy airport until his flight was called, and then he boarded the plane and started his trip to New York, leaving his heart behind in Ohio.

***

Olivia decided Chris must have gone to his apartment, so she hurried over to his place to confront him about abandoning her at the church. She knocked on the door, and then waited for him to answer.

When he didn't come to the door, she started screaming and pounding on the door. "If you don't let me in, I'm going to have my father foreclose on your grandfather's loans," she yelled, forgetting about the written agreement she'd signed preventing such action.

When he still didn't answer, she started pounding harder on the door. "Chris, don't push me on this," she shrieked at the door.

"Excuse me," a young woman said behind her.

Olivia spun around to face the voice. "What do you want?" she uttered hatefully.

"I just wanted to tell you that Chris had a flight out at eleven today."

"And just how do you know that? Are you that bitch he's been sleeping with?"

Janet took a step back at the venom of her question. "No, I'm his neighbor," she replied, wishing she hadn't spoken to her. "My husband works at the same company, and they went to New York on business."

"Do you happen to know where he's staying?" Olivia asked sweetly, thinking the other woman would simply give her the information she requested.

The woman laughed. "Why don't you call Chris and ask him yourself, as I'm not about to give out his personal information out to someone I don't know."

"He won't mind, you see, I'm his wife."

Janet knew about Chris's forced marriage, as her husband had told her about the blackmail scheme. Seeing the woman in action, she understood why

Chris hadn't told this woman anything about his trip. "Then I'm sure he'll be calling you to tell you where he is," she stated with fake pleasantry.

Olivia was furious at this woman's rude behavior, but if she was going to get anywhere with her, she had to play by her rules. "Can you at least tell me when he's due to come back?"

An ornery smile covered Janet's face as a magnificent idea had suddenly come to her. "Since you asked so nicely, I'll tell you," she replied in a malicious tone, which was lost on Olivia. "He's due back at the end of the month."

"What?" Olivia exclaimed loudly. "This is only the second; you're telling me they're going to be gone for a whole month? Why are they going to be gone for so long?"

"There's some trouble regarding his company. I hate it too, as my husband won't be back until then either."

Olivia gave her a dirty look. "Like I give a damn how this trip affects you." She then turned and stomped off, letting the door slam behind her as she stormed out to the parking lot.

***

After Olivia march off, Janet returned to her apartment and called the hotel the two men were staying at in New York.

Chris was closer to the phone, so he answered it. "Hello?"

"Chris, just the man I was looking for."

Chris laughed. "I have you know that I'm a newly wedded man," he replied teasingly.

"I just meet that lovely new wife of yours and you have my condolences."

"What did she want?" he asked, as it didn't surprise him that Olivia had gone to his apartment.

"She wanted to know where you were, but I wouldn't tell her, so then she asked when you were due home."

"What did you tell her?" he asked, assuming she'd given her the time and date of his flight home.

"I told her that you would be home at the end of the month."

Chris chuckled at her comment, as their meeting would be over tomorrow. "Thanks Janet. How can I ever repay you?"

"Just keep an eye on my husband and don't let him wander off with another woman."

"John loves you too much to be unfaithful."

"Thanks Chris. So tell me, what are you going to do with all those extra days?"

"See if I can get hold of the woman I love and spend some time with her."

"I wish you luck."

"Your husband is giving me some dirty looks, so I better hand over the phone to him."

After John got off the phone with his wife, Chris called Elena. He begged her to let him come see her for a few days, and was heartbroken when she told him no. He understood why she refused to see him, but it didn't soften the blow of her refusal.

That night as the two men were getting ready for bed, the phone rang. Thinking it would be for John, Chris let him answer it and was confused when his friend handed him the phone.

He looked at his friend with panic in his eyes. "Who is it?" he asked, keeping his hands at his side, as he was afraid it was Olivia on the other end.

"Someone you'll want to talk to. I'm going to go for a walk, so take your time."

"Hello?"

"Chris," Elena started, afraid he would hang up on her because of their earlier conversation.

"Elena, what's wrong? Are you hurt or sick?" he asked as soon as he knew who was on the phone.

"I've changed my mind about seeing you before you go home. I need you and I don't care if I'm the other woman."

"Tell me what's wrong."

"Not over the phone."

"I'll be there as soon as I can."

Chris worried all the way to Ohio, and as soon as he stepped into Elena's apartment, she told him that they were going to have a baby. Chris was ecstatic as well as disappointed, as being married to Olivia; he wouldn't be able to be a full time father to their child. The two made plans for Chris to fly to see her every other week, as they couldn't stand to be apart, that and they didn't want Olivia to get suspicious.

***

After spending almost four weeks with the woman, he loved, Chris returned to Kansas City, and he had just unpacked his suitcase when he heard a knock at the door. When he opened it, he was surprised to see

Olivia there, wondering how she knew he was home. After a moment, he realized Olivia must have someone keeping an eye on his apartment, which meant he had to be careful whenever he flew out to see Elena.

"My father is furious of how you've treated me."

"You told me I had to married you, you never said I had to live with you," he said, forcing himself to sound sincere.

"Of course you have to live with me, you're my husband," she stated angrily, so furious with him that her nostrils flared.

"Not by choice," he said coldly.

"I won't allow you to embarrass me in front of my family and friends," she said, putting each of her hand on her hips.

"It's kind of late to be worrying about that."

She gave him a perplexed look. "What is that suppose to mean?"

"When there's no baby, I'm sure all those people you told that I'd gotten you pregnant, will soon know you lied about me knocking you up. Then they'll know what kind of woman you really are."

"And what kind is that?" she asked sarcastically.

"A scheming blackmailing bitch," he stated.

Olivia was so livid at his name-calling that she slapped his face as hard as she could. "Well this scheming blackmailing bitch will tell everyone that I had a miscarriage, due to being separated from my husband for practically a month," she uttered, still angry for what he'd just called her. "Just so we're on the same page here, don't you dare speak to me like that ever again, you understand?"

"I'll speak to you any way I want," he said as he rubbed his cheek.

"Fine, have it your way. When my father forecloses on your grandfather's farm, you just remember this conversation," she yelled loudly

His eyes turned cold. "Still threatening me?"

"You think you won by leaving me before we had our wedding night, but I'm going to make you suffer for your actions."

"You signed a contract to the fact that your father can't foreclose as long as we're married. Since you're retracting your word, I guess I just have to have our marriage annulled."

His statement caused her blood to turn cold. "You wouldn't dare."

"Don't push me, or you'll find out just what I'll dare to do."

"I won't have Daddy foreclose on your grandfather's loan, but I know all about your romance with Elena. So you better believe me when I tell you that I can make her life a living hell." And she would, that is as soon as she found out the woman's last name, but she didn't tell Chris that.

So far, the private investigator she hired to spy on Chris hadn't come up with anything regarding Elena. Of course, with Elena living out of town, unless the investigator followed Chris to Ohio, he wouldn't ever catch Chris being unfaithful to his wife.

He began to boil at her threat. "You keep Elena out of this."

"You're going to have to choose me or else...," she uttered angrily.

"Or what?" He wasn't worried about her threat, just wanted to know what she was thinking.

"Or I'll smear her name so badly no one will have anything to do with her."

He laughed. "What will that accomplish?" he asked, watching her closely in anticipation of her answer.

"That I've won the war."

"You can coerce me to stay married to you, but you can't force me to love you."

"We'll see about that, but first you have to move in with me."

"Why should I have to live with you?" he asked just to tick her off.

"Since other husbands and wives live together, so will we."

"I'm not living with you."

"I may not be able to do anything about your grandfather's loan, but I can do other things to make his life miserable."

"I'm not living with your parents."

"And I'm not moving into this dingy apartment, so we'll have to buy a house. I know just the one I want."

With her father's help, Olivia bought a mansion, and if Chris had known what she planned to buy, he would have put his foot down. The only good thing about the size of the house was that it was large enough for him to have a suite to himself, seeing his wife only at meal times.

Since the loan wasn't in his name, that meant he didn't have to make mortgage payments, and the day he could leave her, he could do it without worrying about what to do with this monstrosity.

***

They had been married for three months, and so far, their marriage hadn't been consummated, as Chris kept his bedroom door locked at night to keep his wife from joining him in his bed. Olivia knew in order to keep her husband from having their marriage annulled any time he pleased; she had to have a wedding night, so she came up with a foolproof plan.

That night just as he finished eating his dinner, Chris started feeling unsteady and lightheaded. Thinking he may be coming down with something, he went on to bed. He locked his door as usual, removed all of his clothes, and crawled into bed. Two minutes after lying down, he was sound asleep, not even waking when Olivia crawled in bed with him.

Unaware that Olivia had changed the lock on his bedroom door, Chris made love to the warm woman in his arms, as he was dreaming Elena was in bed with him. It wasn't until the next morning when he looked over at his bed partner, that he realized he was in trouble. For instead of seeing the woman he loved, it was Olivia smiling at him.

"What are you doing here?"

"Having my wedding night." She gave him a coy smiled. "I thought it was best if I made sure there wouldn't be an annulment."

It was then that he realized he'd been drugged, and since she was naked, she'd most likely had indeed consummated their marriage.

"How did you get in here?"

"I changed the locks, put something in your dinner to enable me to have my way with you, and then just waited for the right moment."

Instead of ordering her to leave his room, he got out of bed. Not caring about her loud moaning of desire at seeing his bare backside, he grabbed all of his clothes and walked to his bathroom. After shutting and locking the door, he got dressed, and then he opened the door and walked out of the room, continuing until he was out of the house. As he drove to work, swore he would never trust that woman as long as he lived.

That evening, Chris put a slide lock on the door, so he could bolt her out of his room. Not only didn't they ever share a bed again, Chris refused to eat her cooking, either eating something on the way home or fix a meal for himself at home.

Their one night together not only prevented Chris from ever getting an annulment from Olivia, but it also started a baby growing in her belly.

***

The next two months were awful for Chris, married to a woman he hated, and longing for a woman he loved, but couldn't have. When Olivia told Chris she was expecting, he was furious, as this only tightened the rope she had around his neck. Now even if his grandfather paid off his loan tomorrow, if he wanted his child in his life, he would have to stay married to Olivia.

Not wanting to keep any secrets from Elena, he immediately called her and told her the news. Since he had already explained to her about the night Olivia had drugged him, she wasn't surprised by this announcement, only saddened to know that Olivia was giving him a child three months after their child was born.

* * *

Elena called him when her ultra sound was scheduled, so he was there when they learned they were going to have a baby boy. When Elena went into labor, she called him that it was time and Chris booked the first flight out, hoping he would be able to be with the woman he loved when she gave birth to their son.

Chris not wanting Olivia to know what he was up to, he snuck out the back of his office building, and hurried to the airport. Just before he boarded the plane, he called Olivia to tell her that he had a business meeting out of town, and wasn't sure when he would be back.

Chris arrived just in time to see the birth their little boy, which Elena named Colin after Chris' deceased father. Holding his son in his arms and knowing the child and the woman he loved couldn't be a regular family; he hated himself even more for giving in to Olivia's blackmail.

Chris wanting to be in his son's life as much as possible flew to Cincinnati every Wednesday, spend one night with them, and then return to Kansas City the next morning. It wasn't a perfect solution for them, but at least he had Elena and Colin in his life. And since Olivia assume Elena lived nearby; she didn't question her husband's trip on the night Colin was born, or any of the ones he took over the next two decades.

***

Three months after his son Colin was born, Olivia went into labor. Once they were at the hospital, she expected her husband to be with her in the delivery room, but he refused, as he wasn't going act like the loving husband in front of the doctor and all the nurses just for appearance sake.

Hurt by his actions, she named him the baby, Monroe Fraser just to spite Chris, but it didn't bother him, as he didn't plan to care for the child.

After Monroe's birth, Fraser went to see Chris at his office. "Why didn't you go into the labor room with Olivia during the birth of your child?"

Chris just laughed. "As you recall, Olivia lied about me getting her pregnant before we were married and just because Olivia gave birth to this child, it doesn't prove I'm the father. She led me to believe we had sex once, but since I was drugged at the time, I can't swear that the deed had actually happened. Because of that fact, I'm having the baby's DNA tested to confirm the child's even mine," he said, giving his father-in-low a smug look.

"You wouldn't dare," Fraser shouted.

Chris didn't acknowledge his comment. "Blackmail or not, if I find out the boy isn't mine, I'll renounce him as mine and divorce Olivia, as I refuse to be Olivia's patsy," Chris angrily told his father-in-law.

Fraser taking offence to his comment that there was a possibility that the child wasn't his plowed his fist into his son-in-law's face.

Chris simply laughed. His words to his father-in-law had been braved ones, but knowing the way his luck had been going since meeting Olivia, he was sure the child would turn out to be his. If that was so, then he would have to remain married to the Wicked Witch of Evil until the child was eighteen. And sure enough, Monroe did turn out to be his biological son. Accepting that fact, Chris became the father any son would be proud to have.

***

Slowly the years passed, and the bond that formed between father and son became so strong, it caused

Olivia to be jealous of their close relationship. So envious, she consistently tried to break the tie they had between them, but all she ended up doing was making Monroe detest his own mother.

With Olivia still unaware that Chris had a son with Elena, he continued to visit Cincinnati each week to see his son and the woman he love. He spent as much time with the boy as possible, but since he couldn't risk Olivia finding out about his son's existence or that he was still seeing Elena, he never stayed more than two days before returning home.

When Monroe turned five, Chris decided it was time for the two brothers to meet for the first time, so he told Olivia he wanted to take on Monroe a father-son trip. Not wanting her to go with them, he told her they were going camping, an activity he knew she disliked and then the two Regan males took off for Ohio for a week.

As they stood outside Elena's apartment, Chris knelt down and took hold of his young son's hands into his. "Monroe, you can't ever tell your mommy about the little boy you're about to meet. And I do mean *never*," he stressed, as he looked the boy in the eye.

"Why?" he asked, his eyes wide with confusion at his father's words.

"Because, your mommy will be very mad at me if she finds out about him. Then not only won't you ever see the little boy again, she may even take you away from me." He hated telling Monroe that, but he had to instill into him how important it was that Olivia never knew about Colin.

"But why?" he asked tearfully, afraid he might lose his father.

"Because the little boy is your half-brother, but your mother doesn't know about him."

"I have a brother?" His eyes lit up. "I always wanted a brother. Where did you get him?"

"He's my son, the same as you are, but he has a different mommy than you do. Now promise not to tell your mommy as she can't ever know he's my son."

"I promise I won't ever tell anyone I have a brother," Monroe said in a whisper. And he kept his word; never saying a word to anyone that Colin was his brother, including the woman he married twenty years later.

***

As Monroe grew older, he came to understand that his parents didn't have a normal marriage, as he never saw them hug, kiss, say a nice word to each other, or sleep in the same room. When he was fifteen, he finally got up the nerve to ask his father why he married his mother, as he knew there wasn't any love between them.

Chris explained about Olivia's threats to have her father foreclose on his grandfather Albert's property if he didn't marry her. Also, because he didn't want to lose Monroe, he'd stay married to his mother all these years so he could be close to his youngest son.

Monroe was shocked by his mother ploy regarding his father. If he had his way, his father would have divorced his mother and married Elena, the only woman to show him what a real mother's love was like. Monroe's only comment to his father was he wanted him to divorce his mother and marry the woman he loved as soon as Grandpa Albert's loan was paid off.

Chris told his son, he couldn't wait until the day he was free to marry Elena, the only woman he'd ever love. Each day that passed, was one more day closer in being able to do just that. Chris kept expecting Elena to tell him she'd fallen in love with someone else, but she never did.

Once he asked her why she was still involved with him, she told him it was because he was her soul mate, the only man for her. Someday their day would come, and when it did, they planned to live happily ever after.

CHAPTER ONE

Albert Regan loved his horse ranch, but he was getting too old to run the place by himself any longer. His old joints ached and complained anytime he got on one of his horses and there was the worry that once he was on the horse, he could fall and break a hip or something worst such as his neck.

Since his grandson, Monroe wouldn't be able to help until he got out of the Navy, which was still months away, Albert decided it was time to hire some help. But before Albert could to anything regarding finding that help, he found out that the three Sims children across the road were about to be lose their home due to the death of their father.

Jayna and Christa, fraternal twins, were twenty-two, and their brother Grayson was twenty. They weren't young children any longer, but with all three of them in college, they weren't ready to be out on the own just yet. Their father, Howard had a large insurance policy, but none of them could touch it until Grayson turned twenty-one, so it wouldn't be any help to them for several more months.

Howard had done the best he could for his family, and would have done more if he hadn't gotten sick and died. The children's mother, Rose had died the year before, and since there were so many medical bills between their parents' illnesses, the children decided to put up the family ranch for sale in order to bury their father and pay off the medical bills. In doing so, it left them without any place to live.

The family had been Albert's neighbor long before the children were born. And since Howard and Chris had been good friends since they were young boys, there wasn't any way Albert would allow the man's children to be homeless when he was able to help.

Unbeknown to the three Sims, Albert bought their ranch, his plan being that when the family received their inheritance, he would sell the ranch back to them.

Of course, this time when he took out a mortgage, he didn't go to any bank that Fraser Reinhardt had any connections with, as he didn't want any more trouble coming from that area.

When Chris married Olivia, Albert was suspicious why he would marry a woman he seemed to hate. He hired a good friend to investigate into the situation, and wasn't surprise to learn that Olivia had blackmailed Chris because of his mortgage loan at Fraser's bank. Albert felt horrible at knowing his grandson had given up so much because of him, so anytime he had an extra dollar, he paid it towards his loan.

Since Albert had only ten thousand left on the loan on his place, when he took out the loan for the Sims' place, he increased the amount of it so he could pay off his loan at Fraser's bank. And since the check to pay off his place was in the works, he would soon be able to tell his grandson to divorce *that horrible woman* he'd married and get on with his life.

When Albert returned from signing all the paperwork, he went over to the Sims' ranch and told the three siblings he wanted them to move in with him. They thanked him, but said they didn't have any money to pay their way.

Albert just laughed, saying their payment for living with him would be to help him run his place. Relieved to have a place to live where the three of them could be together and still go to school, they packed their personal belongings, and moved across the street, storing their furniture and any other items they didn't need in Albert's barn. The last thing the three Sims children did together before leaving their home for good was to bring their horses and cattle over, adding them to the rest of Albert's stock.

Albert didn't tell them that he had bought their place or that he was fixing it up, as he wanted it to be a surprise. The place didn't need much work other than a good coat of paint and a new roof, which Albert planned to have done over the next few weeks.

***

When Jayna and her siblings arrived at Albert's home, she knocked on the screen door. As they waited for Albert to answer the door, Jayna could see Marty, Monroe's black and white cat sleeping in a sunny spot just inside the door.

A pain filled her, as her cat, Jasmine had been killed the month before. The cat had been the runt of the litter, had a funny tooth and a damaged tail, but Jayna still had loved her.

When Albert came to the door, he was smiling. As he opened the door, he told the three siblings they didn't need to knock, as this was now their home.

After Jayna entered the house, Marty came over to rub against her leg, and she leaned down and picked up the cat. When she started stroking him, the young cat began purring in her arms, causing her to smile, the first one in days.

"Marty's glad to have someone other than me to take care of him. Don't be surprised if he decides to sleep in your room."

Jayna looked up at him, with a worried look on her face. "Do you mind?"

"I'm more a dog person," Albert told her. "The cat actually belonged to Monroe, but when he'd gone into the service, his mother refused to let Marty stay at their home, so the cat came to stay with me until Monroe returns home."

Jayna looked around the room. "Where's Toby by the way?"

"He's outside chasing squirrels."

Jayna laughed. "Poor little squirrels."

Last year Albert had moved to the downstairs bedroom, as the stairs were too much for an eighty-year-old man with arthritis to climb anymore. So that left the three bedrooms upstairs empty.

Albert laughed. "Now let's get the three of you settled. I'm putting you girls in my old room and Grayson in Monroe's room."

Jayna tried to keep her thoughts away from Albert's great grandson, as she was fallen in love with Monroe Regan when she was only thirteen. That was the year Monroe and his friend, Colin Sparkman from Ohio had spent the whole summer with Albert, and the three Sims were often seen with Monroe and his friend.

As Jayna spent time with the two boys, she thought Colin reminded her somewhat of Monroe, not only by his looks, but also by some of his mannerisms, but she never commented on it as she assumed it was just her imagination.

One night as the five sat around fire pit, Monroe told them stories of his parent's loveless marriage, saying that he would only marry for love. Colin had agreed with him, adding that he wouldn't let anything or anyone come between him and the woman he loved.

Colin's words had Jayna wishing Monroe would feel that way about her some day when they were older. As they got older, she saw less and less of Monroe and whenever Colin came back to Albert's place, she didn't get a chance to see him, as the boys didn't want the girls tagging along with them.

***

That night when the two girls went to bed, Marty jumped in bed with Jayna. As she started stroking him, she thought of everything she'd lost recently and began crying. How she missed her parents, thinking if they hadn't died, she would be sleeping in her own bed tonight, but that wouldn't ever happen again.

Christa got out of bed and crawled in bed with her sister. "Jayna, it's going to be okay," she said, putting her arm around her sister to comfort her.

Jayna looked over at her. "How can you say that? We don't have parents anymore, we've lost our home, and if it hadn't been for Albert, we would be living out on the streets."

"The three of us *are* together, and somehow we will get through Dad's death, just like we did Mom's."

Jayna took hold of her sister's hand. "I was thinking about quitting college and getting a full time job."

"No, you aren't going to quit school with only one semester left," Christa told her.

"You're at least bringing in some money from your part time job, I on the other hand, aren't even doing that much."

"That's because you're taking harder classes than I am."

"What if Grayson doesn't get a scholarship next semester?"

"After graduation, we'll be getting full time jobs. Once you have your nursing degree, you'll be able to help, and if Grayson doesn't get a scholarship, we'll both help him financially so he can stay in school."

"I guess you're right as usual."

Christa laughed. "Are you going to be okay now?"

"Yes, thanks for comforting me."

"That's what sisters are for."

Though she and Monroe weren't involved romantically, she had been writing to him since he joined the Navy, keeping him informed about what's happening in her life. She had written to him about her father's death, but not about moving in with his great grandfather. As Jayna lay there, she said a prayer that Monroe would stay safe, closed her eyes and fell asleep.

After their father's funeral, their life slowly returned to some sort of daily routine, as the three Sims children returned to their college classes and Christa returned to her night job. And now instead of doing daily chores around their place, they took care of Albert's place.

***

One day a week after moving in with Albert, while the three Sims were out checking the fences around his place, the old man walked over to their homestead to see how the repairs were coming along on their house. He was still out when the three returned to the house, but they didn't think anything about him not being there, as often he wasn't.

When suppertime came around, Jayna started fixing their evening meal. When it was ready, she thought about waiting to eat until Mr. Regan returned home, but her family was hungry, so they went ahead and ate without him.

When it grew dark outside, the family began to worry about Mr. Regan. Not only didn't they know where he'd gone, but because he hadn't taken his car, they didn't know if he was with someone or had simply gone out for a walk. Then before they knew it, it was too dark to go looking for him on his land. They kept expecting him to show up, but when the clock struck midnight, the three went on to bed, but none of them slept well for worrying about Albert.

At first light, the three Sims got on their horses and started searching the property for the old man, but they didn't have any luck in finding him. When noontime came and they still couldn't find him, they returned to the house, and Jayna called Kent Powell, the sheriff.

When they heard a truck, pulling in front of the house, Jayna ran to the door hoping it was Albert returning home. When she saw Kent getting out of his truck, she told her siblings who was here and they rushed outside to meet him.

"Thanks for coming so quickly," Jayna said.

"I guess you still haven't heard from Albert?"

"No, not a word. What are we going to do?" Christa asked tearfully.

"Jasper Miller is bringing his coon dog. Once he gets a good scent of Albert, I'm sure we'll be able to find him." Kent squeezed her hand. "So quit worrying."

"I'll go get one of his shirts," Jayna offered.

"Jayna, wait a minute," he called.

She turned to look at him. "What?"

"Have any of you called Chris about his grandfather?"

"I did, and his witch of a wife told me that he was out of town and refused to call him or to give me the number of where he was."

Kent had to bite his tongue, as he had to agree with Jayna's assessment of Chris' wife, as he'd had his share of her rude comments from her. "Do you have any other numbers for him?"

"Albert may have one, but if he does, it isn't in his address book."

"We'll find Albert first, and then when we call Chris, we'll have something good to tell him about his grandfather."

Jayna ran into the house to get the shirt and just as she returned to the front porch, Jasper, with his dog Roscoe, pulled into the driveway.

As soon as Roscoe got Albert's scent, he started down the driveway. When he ran straight across the road, the three Sims looked at each other, as they were confused to why the dog was going towards their old place. They knew someone had bought it the day after it was listed, but they hadn't seen anyone move in as of yet.

The group quickly followed, and when they came upon the still body of Albert laying on his back inside the barn, the two sisters began sobbing thinking their good friend; the wonderful man who had rescued them was dead.

Kent hurried over to Albert, knelt down next to him, and reached out to check for a pulse. Expecting to find the old man dead, he was quite surprised when Albert opened his eyes and looked up at him.

"You old geezer, what in the hell are you doing over here without anyone knowing where you went?"

"Kent, could you call for some help before you ball me out?" he asked with a slight smile.

"Only for you I will. Tell me what hurts."

"It's my chest. I think it's my heart."

As Kent called for an ambulance, the two girls ran to Albert's side.

"We were so worried about you," Jayna said, as she took hold of his hand, her tears ran down her face.

Christa took off her jacket, made a pillow out of it, and then put in under his head. "What are you doing over here? If it hadn't been for Roscoe, we wouldn't have found you until the buzzards were circling your body."

Albert smiled at her. "I love you too."

"Well? Are you going to tell us or not?"

"I own the place," he said as he looked at the two girls.

"What do you mean you own the place?" Jayna asked.

"I bought it so you three wouldn't lose your home. I plan to sell it back to you when your father's life insurance paid out."

The two girls bent down and each kissed one of his cheeks.

After the ambulance came and took Albert away, with the group following to the hospital, Kent walked across the road to Albert's home to see if he could find a number for Chris. When he saw Elena's number, he took a chance Chris may be with her, as he knew she was the woman his friend loved.

"Hello?"

"Elena, this Kent. Is Chris there by any chance?"

"Yes, he is, just a moment."

"Kent, what's wrong?" Chris asked, as he knew his friend wouldn't have called unless it was an emergency.

"Chris, we've had a bit of trouble here and your grandfather is on his way to the hospital."

Hearing his friend's words, Chris assumed the worst. "How bad is he?"

"I'm not sure, but the Sims family went to the hospital to be with him."

"I'll be home on the next flight."

"Take care."

***

When Chris arrived at his grandfather's hospital room, he was greatly relieved to see Albert sitting up, with the three Sims children sitting on the bed talking to him. After they all spoke, the Sims family left so Chris could speak with his grandfather alone.

"Grandpa, maybe it's time to sell the place."

"No, I promised the place to Monroe."

"Are you sure he still wants the place?"

"I'll tell you what I'll do. I'll ask him, and if he doesn't want my place, I'll sell it and we'll all move to the Sims' ranch," he said with a smile, knowing Chris wasn't going to like that answer any better.

"Grandpa how is that going to make any difference?" he asked gently.

"I'm not moving to a nursing home," he stated angrily.

Chris gave his grandfather a perplexed look. "When did I ever say I was going to put you in a home?"

"You haven't, but I know that a lot of my friends' families have done that to them."

"I'm not asking you to move somewhere you don't want to be, only one that doesn't require so much work."

"Let me check with Monroe, and then I'll make a decision."

Chris simply nodded in agreement, as he knew it wouldn't do any good to try to get his grandfather to sell his home if he wasn't ready to do so.

***

After spending a week in the hospital, Albert was coming home with a list the doctor had given him of things he could and couldn't do. When Chris brought him home, he wanted to tell his grandfather that having the Sims family was too much on him, but knew they filled his home with love and affection, giving his life purpose again. Not only that, but they were there to keep an eye on him, thus preventing Albert from overdoing.

CHAPTER TWO

When Monroe, who was now stationed in Louisiana, got his next leave, he called his father.

"Hello?"

"Dad, I'm calling to let you know I'm coming home on a short leave. I should be arriving around three tomorrow afternoon and wanted to know if you can pick me up at the airport."

"Your mother is going to be thrilled."

"Mom isn't going to like it when I tell her I'm here to look for an apartment."

"You're getting out?"

"I still have another month on my enlistment, but I want to have a place ready for when I do get out."

"Your mother has to accept the fact you're a grown man and don't want to live at home any longer. Maybe you and Colin could share his apartment," Chris said, as his other son was moving to Kansas City next week.

"We could, but my plans include marriage."

"I see," he said. Chris didn't need to ask whom the woman might be, as he knew how his younger son felt about Jayna.

"How are Jayna, Christa, and Grayson doing?" Monroe's heart went out to Jayna and her family, as had to be hard to lose their last parent. He'd fallen in love with Jayna so many summers ago, but then so had Colin.

The two brothers never talked about how they each felt about Jayna, as it was a touchy subject. And for the next few summers whenever Colin came to spend time at Albert's ranch, Monroe made sure he kept his brother away from Jayna.

Monroe never told Jayna how he felt, as she had college and he wanted to serve his country before he could think about having a serious relationship with her. When he'd joined the military, she kissed him on the cheek, told him to be careful, and had faithfully written to him each week for the past three years.

"Good so far. Grandpa says all three of them are helping him around the place."

"Has their place sold yet?"

"According to your grandpa, he bought it."

"What?" he exclaimed loudly. "Why did he do that if he can't take care of his own place any longer?"

"He did it so someday they can move back to their ranch."

"That was sweet of the old guy, but how does that affect your marriage to Mom?"

"He says he took out a loan at a different bank," Chris told him.

"That's good, but how is he affording to pay on two loans?"

"Good question."

"You haven't asked him about it?"

"No, I haven't."

"Dad, you need to know how much longer you have to stay married to Mom. If you don't ask him, I will."

"I will, but not today."

"When?"

"Monroe, I'll do it when the time is right."

"You've been unhappily married to my mother long enough; it's time for you to have a life with Elena."

"Monroe, I promise I'll ask him before the month is over. I'll see you when you arrive at the airport."

Monroe realized that conversation was over; so he let it die a peaceful death. "Sure. Love you, Dad. Bye."

"Bye and I love you too, son."

As Chris disconnected their call, he realized his son was right. It was time to start living his own life and the first thing he was going to do was go talk to his grandfather. Wanting to do it in person, he left work and drove over to his place.

"Grandpa, are you here?" Chris called into the house.

"I'm in the kitchen," Albert replied.

When Chris entered the kitchen, his grandfather was sitting at the table with a cup of hot tea looking well. "You're looking spry, how are you feeling?"

"I feel wonderful, nothing like having loved ones in my home again."

"So it's going well with the Sims family?"

"I don't do any of the cooking, the housekeeping, or the laundry. I just sit back and take it easy." Albert looked at his grandson, and seeing a special something in his expression, he knew Chris had something he wanted to talk to him about. "Out with it, as that look on your face is telling me you need to ask me something. Do you want to tell me what it is or do I have to guess?"

Chris sat down next to him. "Monroe is coming home to start looking for an apartment as his enlistment is up next month."

"He's such a good boy. Both your boys are."

"Thanks, Grandpa. Did Colin call you about the job he has lined up here?"

"Yes, he did. He told me he found an apartment and will be moving here as soon as he can get everything packed. I can't believe you've been able to keep Colin's existence a secret from Olivia all these years."

"I was sure she would find out about him after Monroe met his brother for the first time, as he kept going on about how he wanted to see his new friend, Colin again. When Olivia asked him who the boy was, Monroe simply told her he was someone he met in Cincinnati on our trip."

"It was good of Elena to allow Colin to spend the summers here, as a lot of mothers wouldn't want their child to be gone that long from them."

"She felt it was important for the brothers to have that time together, as well for Colin to have time with me. If it hadn't been for those summers, I don't think the boys would be as close as they are today."

"I think you're right. Those yearly camping trips with Colin and Elena gave him a taste of what a real family was like."

Chris just sat there looking at the table, not sure how to bring up the subject on his new loan. "Grandpa, how are you going to be able to pay on two mortgages?"

"I've taken out an additional amount on the new loan so I can pay off the mortgage on this place, and once I do, you can divorce Olivia, as she won't have any hold on you any longer."

Chris was surprised by his grandfather's statement. "Grandpa, you knew?"

"Yes, I've known from the beginning that I'm the reason you had to marry Olivia. I tried my darnedest to pay it off early, but it's taken a while."

"I've never blamed you for having to marry Olivia, as if we hadn't gotten married, then I wouldn't have Monroe in my life." Chris went to his grandfather and pulled him up into a hug. "I love you Grandpa."

"I love you too. Just do me a favor and divorce that bitch."

Chris laughed. "I will as soon as possible."

CHAPTER THREE

When Monroe entered his Great Grandfather's house, he didn't see anyone, but hearing a sound coming from the kitchen, he headed in that direction. When he stepped into the room, he saw Jayna looking at him, with a surprised look on her face. He wished he could kiss her, but first he had to find the nerve to tell her how he felt about her.

"Jayna, how are you doing?" he asked, hoping his voice didn't give away his desire for her.

Jayna was puzzled by the sound of longing in his voice. "I'm doing better thanks to your family."

"Are Christa and Grayson here?" Monroe asked as he moved closer to her.

"Christa is at work and Grayson's with some friends studying for finals."

"Is my Great Grandpa here?" he asked, as he looked around the room. He smiled as he thought of the man and all the wonderful memories he'd had in this room over the years.

"He went to take his afternoon medicine."

"How's school going for you?" he asked as he moved closer to her.

"A bit rough lately, but it's almost over," she said, glad he was home for good.

"I'm sure losing your father and your home has been hard on you all."

"Yes, but Albert has made things better for us."

"I wish I could do something to ease your pain," he uttered, hoping the longing he had for her hadn't come out in his voice.

Jayna smiled at him. "A hug would be nice."

Monroe just stared at her, as he was afraid that if he touched her, he wouldn't ever be able to let go of her.

Jayna was confused by the way he looked at her, as it was as if he didn't want to touch her. Tears filling her eyes, she started to turn away, but when she felt his hand touch her arm, she turned to look back at him.

"Jayna, I didn't want to tell you this yet, but I can't put it off any longer."

"Tell me what?" she asked softly, frightened he was going to tell her he had a woman in his life.

"I'm in love with you. If I hug you, I'm liable to kiss you."

A smile covered her face. "I think a hug would be wonderful, as I feel the same way about you."

Monroe threw his arms around her and drew her to him, but forced himself to go slow, as he moved his lips closer to hers. The desire that surged through him when their lips met was more than he'd been expecting, and before he knew it, his arms tightened around her.

The kiss continued until they heard someone clearing their throat, which caused them to jump apart. Breathing hard, they looked at the person who had barge in on them.

Albert smiled at the disorientated couple. "Am I interrupting?" he asked with fake innocence.

"Grandpa, Jayna was welcoming me home," Monroe muttered, while trying to keep from blushing.

"I would say that she's glad to see you."

Jayna's face reddened at Albert's words, and she looked down at her hands that were tightly griped together. "I'll let you visit Albert in private," she uttered, then rushed out of the room before either man could stop her.

"I didn't mean to scare her off," Albert told Monroe.

"I think she was embarrassed at being caught kissing."

"There isn't anything wrong with the two of you kissing."

"I know, but I sort of surprised her."

Albert patted Monroe's shoulder. "You'll be good for her."

Monroe smiled at him. "Thanks Grandpa."

***

During Monroe visit, his mother never asked if he was happy or if there was a woman in his life, all she wanted to know when he was going to get out of the service, so he could join her father's company. Since sitting in a business suit all day, didn't appeal to him, the last place he would be working would be at his grandfather's office.

While in the service, Monroe had gone to school to be an electrician, and unbeknown to his mother, his father had gotten him a job doing work he loved and he would start the week after he got out of the service.

His mother also assumed he would be moving back home when he got out, but he was moving in the same apartment complex as Colin. He was so relieved that he wouldn't have to live with his mother ever again as his new apartment would be ready the week before he got released from the service.

Once Colin was settled in his apartment, he was going to furnish Monroe's apartment so it would be all ready for him to move in when he got out of the Navy. He and Colin had talked about a lot of things the last time they'd spoken, but Monroe hadn't told his brother that he planned to ask Jayna to marry him once he was home for good.

Finally, the day came when Monroe's enlistment was over. He had already made plans for Jayna to pick him up at the airport, and so when he walked out of the walkway, she was standing there waiting for him.

After a breathtaking welcomed hello kiss, they left the airport and started towards his new apartment. He let her drive, as he was too nervous to concentrate for he was going to propose to as soon as they reached his apartment.

The moment they were alone, Monroe took Jayna and pulled her into his arms. He brought his lips down hard on hers, as one hand went to her butt, and the other reached for her breast. His lips left hers, and moving to the side of her face, he kissed her ear. "I want you baby."

Jayna pushed away from him, and then stood there just staring at him, as she waited for her breathing to calm down. "Monroe, I want you too, but I won't have sex with you unless we're married. My family is known to be very fertile, and I refuse to have a baby out of wedlock."

"Then marry me."

Jayna laughed at his statement. "Is this a joke?"

"No, it isn't. We love each other; my family loves you, so why wait?"

"That's not entirely true. Your mother doesn't like me."

He shrugged his shoulders. "Don't let it bother you; she hasn't ever liked any of my friends. It was as if she didn't want to share me with anyone else."

"What about Colin? Didn't she like him?"

"They never met."

Her eyes showed her bewilderment. "You're kidding."

"No, I'm not. Now let's get back to us," he said, as he didn't want to tell her that Colin was his half-brother, instead of just a friend.

"How is your mother going to take it when you tell her that we're getting married?"

"She isn't going to like it, but that's just too bad. This is my life and I'm going to marry the woman I love," Monroe stated boldly for Jayna's sake. They were brave words; for he knew his mother would try to talk him out of marrying Jayna, as she didn't think she was good enough for him. "Have you given any thought about eloping?"

Jayna looked at him, wondering if he was teasing her or not. "Are you serious?"

"Yes, I am."

"Monroe, I want a church wedding with our family and friends present."

He didn't want his mother to interfere in their plans, nor did he want to take away the wedding she wanted, so which one should they choose. "I got it. We'll elope, that way my mother can't stop us from getting married." He put his hand up to prevent her from speaking. "Then when we return, we'll have our church wedding, and no matter what tricks my mother comes up with, it won't do her any good, as it would be too late for her to prevent us from saying our vows in church."

"Do you really think we'll have to elope?"

"Knowing my mother, if we were to tell her we were going to get married, she would find a way to blackmail you into changing your mind."

Jayna laughed as she thought Monroe was joking. When she saw he wasn't smiling, she became worried. "You're serious, aren't you?"

"Yes, there are stories I could tell you about my mother that would make your skin crawl. All I can say about her is she simply isn't a nice person." He didn't say any more about his mother, as Jayna just might ask questions he didn't want to answer.

"Your dad seems to be a great guy."

Monroe nodded. "He's cool."

"Do you love your mother?" she asked softly.

"No. I did when I was younger, but back then I didn't know what kind of person she truly was. As I got older, I realized my mother always got her way, no matter who she had to step on to accomplish it."

"Then why do you have anything to do with her?"

"If I don't, she finds a way to make my father pay for not spending time with her."

"How did your mother take the news about your new job?"

Monroe laughed. "They probably could hear her yelling in St. Louis. Dad told her to butt out of it as I was a grown man, and could make my own decision what I did for a living."

"I bet that didn't go over well with your mother."

"No, but she did backed off. Now let's get back to us."

"Since I don't want your mother to prevent us from getting married, I agree to elope. So now the question is when and where are we going to do it."

"I'll call the airlines to check for the next available flight to Las Vegas."

Jayna giggled. "You can't be serious."

Monroe took her in his arms again. "I'm most definitely am," he said, and then he brought his lips back to hers.

When Monroe's hand started wandering to parts of her body she wasn't ready for him to touch, she pushed away from him. "I don't want to fly to Las Vegas. Certainly there's somewhere here in town we can get married at without your mother finding out about it."

"I don't want anything or anyone interfering with our plans so the wedding has to be our secret."

Jayna just shook her head. "I want to tell Christa and Grayson as I don't like keeping our marriage from my family."

"I promise you can tell them *after* we're married."

"Where will we live if we don't want anyone to know we're married?"

"For now, you'll stay at Albert's and I'll stay in my apartment. This way no one will get suspicious and ask why we have moved in together."

"Okay, but I'm telling you right now, we have better have that wedding as soon as possible, as I don't want to live apart from my husband any longer than I have to."

"Think of it as an adventure," he teased, and then his lips returned to hers.

An hour after landing in Las Vegas, Jayna became Mrs. Monroe Regan, and ten minutes after saying her I do's, she was in bed with her new husband in a nearby hotel room.

***

With no one the wiser of what they'd done, when they returned to town, they went to Monroe's parents' home to announce that they were going to get married. Monroe knew this was going to be an experience, as his mother wasn't going to be one bit happy with his announcement that he was going to marry one of *those* Sims girls.

He found his parents sitting at the dining room table eating lunch. Ready for the explosion, he took hold of Jayna's hand and pulled her with him to the table.

"Mother, Dad, I want you to know that Jayna and I are getting married," he said, and then watched for their expressions to change. Neither of them disappointed him, as Chris smiled with happiness and Olivia frowned in disappointment.

Chris ecstatic by their news, jumped up and rushed over to them, hugging Jayna first, then his son. "Congratulations son, so when is the big day?" he asked happily.

"As soon as we can plan it," Monroe said excitedly.

Olivia gasped at her son's announcement. "Jayna's pregnant," she shrieked, thinking that would be the only reason, her son would marry this girl.

They all turned and stared at Olivia, as they were too shocked by her blunt statement to speak.

"No, Mother, she isn't pregnant. Jayna isn't that kind of girl," he said looking at his mother as to say Olivia was.

Olivia had to find a way to stop them from getting married, and by the looks of things, it had to be quick. "Then what's the rush in getting married. Why don't you date for another couple of months, get to know each other better, then we'll announce your engagement?" Olivia asked, already wondering how much money it would take to get this girl out of her son's life.

"We've known each other since we were kids, and because of that fact, we don't want a long engagement," he told her, smiling to himself, as he knew the great

Olivia Regan was trying to come up with a way to stop them from having that wedding.

Chris was disappointed by his wife's words. Since she always had to have her way, he could almost see the wheels rolling in her head trying to find something that would keep Monroe from marrying the woman he loved. At first, he couldn't imagine what she could possibly do to stop the wedding, but when he realized that Olivia could be planning to use him as a reason for Monroe to cancel the wedding, he swore under his breath.

He would have to talk to Monroe as soon as possible and tell him just to run off and marry the woman he loved, and not worry about him. It didn't matter what Olivia may threatened to do to him, as Chris had already called his lawyer and started divorce proceeding. He had given over twenty-five years of his life for his grandfather and son, and wasn't about to let Olivia do anything to prevent Monroe from marrying the woman *he* loved.

"Mother, we are going to be married with or without you, so it's up to you if you want to be included in our wedding."

Seeing the determined look on her son's face, she gave him a forced smile. "Okay then, let's start planning your wedding," she replied lightly, trying to keep her true feelings from her son. Not only didn't she want her son to marry this woman, she was afraid once their son was married, Chris would leave her. Divorce in her social circle was frown upon, and she wasn't ready to have others talk about her failed marriage.

Monroe wasn't fooled by his mother's calm reply of his declaration, as he knew by this fake acceptance of his announcement to expect something from her when Jayna wasn't with him. "I want the wedding to be in two months."

"Okay, Monroe, we can do that, but if I had five months to plan, I could really make it wonderful for you both," Olivia said to her son, hoping with more time, she could destroy the wedding for good.

"I'll compromise, three months and not a day longer." He handed her a sheet of paper.

"What's this?" she asked as she scanned the names on it.

"These are the people we want invited."

"You got to be kidding," she replied, shocked to see some of the names on the list. "Who is this Colin Sparkman?" she asked, as the name seemed familiar.

"He was the boy I met when I was five and Dad took me camping for the first time."

"I knew his name seemed familiar. Do you think he'd even remember you after all these years?"

Monroe could see that his father was fidgeting, and knew he had to be careful how he answered his mother. "We've seen each other a few times over the years."

"Fine, if you truly have to have him at your wedding."

"I do," he said, as this time he was going to get his way. So happy to know his mother couldn't do anything to prevent their marriage, he almost told her the truth about their situation. It's a shame he hadn't, as the truth would have prevented his mother from being responsible for a tragic incident that happened on the night of their engagement party.

***

After Monroe had taken Jayna back to the ranch and he'd returned to his apartment, he called his brother, as he wanted Colin to hear it from him that he'd married Jayna.

"Hello?"

"Colin, it's your brother."

"Hey, man. Are you all settled in your place?"

"Yes. I want to thank you for all you did to get it ready."

"I was happy to do it. Have you tried out that king size bed yet?" he teased.

"Colin, yes it's great." He had to tell Colin his news, but he just couldn't find the right words to tell him.

"You want to hear something else that's great?"

"Sure, what is it?"

"I got the Jackson's case. The trial is due to start next week." The Jackson murder had been in the papers and on all the television stations, as it was a very high profile case. Colin had been thrill to be asked to be the lawyer to defend the wife who swears that she'd been framed in her husband's murder.

When he'd gotten the Kansas City job offer, he had been so excited. Not only would he be closer to his father and brother, his mother was moving here as soon as she finished working her last two weeks at her job. When his father finally left Olivia and moved in with his mother, then they would all be living in the same apartment complex, but in separate buildings.

In the back of his mind Colin was planning on renewing his acquaintance with Jayna, the girl he'd fallen in love with when he was just a boy. He hadn't gotten a chance to see her yet as he'd been busy, getting settled in his new job, his apartment, helping his mother find a place to live, and then working on Monroe's place to get it ready for when he came home.

"That's wonderful," Monroe responded despondently, as he was worried Colin would disown him as his brother once he told him his news.

Colin noticed Monroe's a lack of excitement. "Monroe, what's wrong? I thought you would be more excited about this."

"I have some news to tell you, but I'm not sure how you're going to take it."

"We're brothers, you can tell me anything. Anything that is except that you're still in love with Jayna," he said jokily. When Monroe didn't respond, Colin knew he'd lost the only woman he'd ever love. "Tell me."

"Jayna and I just got married," he replied, knowing full well how Colin felt about Jayna.

"Well congratulations. Tell Jayna I'm happy for her."

"I'm sorry I didn't tell you before- hand, but we had to get married in secret so my mother couldn't interfere. Jayna is staying out at the ranch until I tell my mother what we've done."

"Don't worry about it, the best man won."

"Colin, you're a good man too. You'll find someone to love."

"I'm sure I will someday," Colin told him, but doubted it, as Jayna was the woman he loved.

After the brothers said good-bye, Colin left his apartment and walked down the block to the local pub. He wasn't planning on getting drunk, just wanted to drown his sorrow a bit with a couple of stiff drinks. He was just about to order his second drink when he noticed a young woman crying at a corner table. Wanting to be helpful, Colin skipped ordering the drink and started for her table.

"Excuse me miss, do you need some help?"

Her sad eyes looked up at Colin, seeing the good-looking man standing in front of her; she assumed the worst about him. "I'm not interested in getting laid," she replied hatefully, "so just leave me alone."

Colin sat down at her table. "Neither am I. Why don't you tell me what's wrong, as maybe I can help?"

"There isn't a thing you can do."

"Let me be the judge of that."

"Fine, if it will get you to leave me alone." She blew her nose on a paper napkin. "I've just come from court, as I had my divorce today. Steve, my ex-husband was given custody of our daughter. Not only that, but I have to pay *him* child support." Her eyes filled with her fury. "The man makes sixty thousand a year, while I bring in less than thirty, how is that fair?"

"Women usually get custody of their children, so what do you think caused the judge to give your daughter to your ex-husband?"

"Gerry had some picture that he doctored that showed a naked woman with my face, in bed with several men. I tried to tell them that pictures weren't of me, but the judge refused to believe me."

"I see." And he did, as Colin had been keeping tabs of this case as it been all in the news. He knew Mark Johnson and Ben Wheeler, the two lawyers on the case as he'd gone to college with them. They had cheated their way through school, so he had first-hand knowledge of what they would do to win a case. Though they were on opposing sides, he bet his last dollar, they were working together to steal this woman's child from her and it was up to him to right this wrong.

"You see, I told you that you couldn't help me," she stated angrily.

"On the contrary, Mrs. Addison, I just may be the man to straighten this out for you."

Pauline was surprise he knew her name. "How do you know who I am?"

"I've been following the trial as it's been in the papers."

"Good for you," she muttered sarcastically.

"I'm a lawyer, and if you hire me, we'll take your ex-husband back to court, but this time you'll come out the winner."

Pauline wanted to believe he was sincere, but it was hard for her to trust men. If he asked for sex in payment for his help, then she'd know for sure he just wanted to use her. "I don't have any money."

"Not a problem. Just seeing Mark Johnson and Ben Wheeler debarred will be enough payment for me."

“Are you a good lawyer?” She was afraid to get her hopes up, but she had to ask.

He smiled at her. “I may be young and haven’t been a lawyer all that long, but I’m one of the best.”

Several days later, the story in the paper of Gerry and Pauline Addison divorce had a different ending. Pauline had her daughter back; the ex-husband would now be paying her child support. Not only that, but he would have to pay a hefty fine and spend two years in jail for what he’d done. The two lawyers were debarred and would serve the same amount of time in the slammer for their part of the scam.

Pauline thanked Colin for all he’d done for her, and when she tried to entice him into her bed, he thanked her for her offer, telling her his heart belonged to someone else.

***

The next day, Chris flew up to Cincinnati to give Elena the news about Monroe getting married.

“Chris, what are you doing here?” she asked nervously, as she was worried something was wrong. Since she would be moving to Kansas City that weekend, she wasn't expecting to see him again until then.

"Aren't you happy to see me?" he teased.

Tears filled her eyes. "I'm always happy to see you, but I didn't think I'd see you until I moved back to Kansas City."

"I couldn't wait that long to see you. Are you going to ask me in?"

She laughed, then grabbed him and pulled him into her home. "Is everything okay at home?"

Chris put his hands on either side of her face, his eyes looking deeply into hers. "I can't believe you have waited for me all these years."

"You're the only man I've ever loved, and we created a son out of that love."

"Have you ever been sorry we didn't have more children?"

"Chris, you know we talked about this years ago, deciding then that Monroe and Colin were enough for us."

"You're right. If it hadn't been for you, Monroe wouldn't have ever had a mother."

"He's a lovely young man. Now are you going to tell me why you're here or are you going to make me guess?"

"My grandfather has paid off his mortgage and Monroe is getting married. Not only that, but my lawyer has started the divorce proceedings from Olivia."

Elena laughed. "I can't believe we're finally going to get married."

"How about the two of us doing the horizontal rumba before I leave?"

"You aren't going to hear me refuse to make love to you, but why can't you stay the whole night?"

"I haven't been asked," he said, as his eyes twinkled with his orneriness.

"Since when do you need to be asked?"

"Never, I hope." His lips moved to hers and the rest of the world was forgotten.

***

While Chris was with the woman he loved, the woman he was married to was up to no good, as she was standing outside an abandon warehouse talking to a shady character named Perry Berger. "I need you to kill someone for me."

"Tell me when and who, and I'll see to it."

"I want you to kill my son's fiancée," she told him as she handed him a photo of Jayna with her son.

Perry didn't even blink an eye when Olivia Regan told him whom to kill, as he'd had enough dealings with her to know better. "When do you want it done?"

"It's to be on the thirtieth. My husband and I will be standing outside the Hilton Hotel, and I want you to shoot Jayna before they enter the building. They're going to announce their engagement that night and I can't allow my son to proclaim to all my friends that he's actually thinking about marry that woman."

"I'll see to it."

Olivia handed Perry an envelope which had five thousand dollars in cash in it, he took it without opening it, and walked back to his car. She smiled, rubbing her hands together, knowing it wouldn't be long before her son was free to marry the woman she'd hand-picked for him.

CHAPTER FOUR

While her sister had Monroe in her life, Christa was lonely, as she hadn't found a man that had captured her heart yet. To help put her through college; she had been working at the local restaurant for the past four years, first as a waitress, and when she turned twenty-one, she moved up to bartender. She'd met a lot of men, most had asked her out on a date, but she always refused, as none of them ever called to her heart.

Maybe once she finished school and was out into the world of professionals, she would find her Mr. Right, as it looked very doubtful she would meet him here. She had just a few more weeks of school, and once graduation was over with, she would be ready to start a full time job. She already had her applications in at several companies as an administrative assistant, and once she was hired, she would quit tending bar.

Three hours after starting her shift, she saw Harrison Ashby, walk in with his usual group of friends. He was a good-looking man, who came in often, but they hadn't ever spoken. She was attracted to him, but hadn't ever waited on them, as Dana, one of her coworkers always took their food and drink orders, saying that someday, Harrison was going to be her husband.

The drunker the group got, the rowdy they became, Christa wanted to have Blackwell, the bouncer, kick the nosily bunch out of the bar, but she remained quiet because she had her application in at Harrison father's law office as his assistant and didn't want anything to ruin her chances at getting the job.

They stayed for another hour, and then they all staggered out into the night, laughing and joking at something one of them said. Five minutes later, Harrison returned alone, and when Christa saw him heading towards her, she became concern.

"Is something wrong Mr. Ashby?"

He was surprise she knew who he was. "No," he said, but instead of saying anything else, he just stared at her.

"Is there something I could get you?"

"I was wondering if you would go out to dinner with me."

For a moment, she was speechless, as his question had surprised her. "I thank you for your lovely offer, at this point and time of my life, I can't." Not wanting him to think she didn't want to go out with him, she knew she needed to say more to him. "But if you come back in two weeks, I would be happy to accept your offer," she said happily, as she smiled at him.

Harrison laughed at her long-winded response, as he nodded his head at her. "I'll see you two weeks from tonight and we'll go out for dinner."

"I'll be waiting."

***

When Harrison arrived two weeks later, he quickly found Christa pouring a beer into a glass and frowned, as he hadn't been expecting to see her working tonight. As he made his way to the bar, he let his anger build. "Why are you working," he yelled out, not caring who was listening.

Christa jumped at the sound of an irate voice behind her. When she turned around and saw Harrison standing there, a gentle smile covered her face. "Well hello to you too."

"I'm sorry. It's been two weeks and so I'm back for our date."

"So you are," she uttered with a light giggle.

"So are you going to go out with me or are you working tonight?" he asked holding his breath as he waited for her answer.

The job with his father's company had fallen through, but it was a blessing in disguise, as five minutes after getting the news, she had a job offer from another company, which offered her better pay and great benefits. Besides, if she were working at Lloyd Ashby's company, it wouldn't look right if she was dating the boss's son.

"I'm just helping out while I waited for you to arrive."

He felt ashamed for his angry tone. "I'm sorry I snapped at you."

"Why did you?" she asked.

"Since you were working, I thought you'd changed your mind about going out with me and I really want to go out with you."

She smiled at his statement. "No, I didn't change my mind. Let me tell Harvey I'm leaving, and then we can leave. Would you like a drink while you wait?"

"How about a glass of water?"

"I think I can do that."

She took a glass, and after filling it with ice, she poured some water into it and then handed it to him. He thanked her, and then she disappeared through some swinging door to the back room.

A few minutes later, when Christa returned, she had tears in her eyes. Harrison seeing the tears became concerned, so he jumped out of his seat, and hurried over to her. "Are you okay?"

She gave him a gentle grin. "I've being working here four years, today was my last shift, and it was hard saying good-bye."

"You're kidding," he said with a bit of anger in his voice.

"No, I'm not," she replied, not sure, why he sounded upset.

"Is that why you told me to come back in two week, you were hoping to be gone when I came back?"

She touched his arm. "No. The reason I told you to come back in two weeks was because I had applied at your father's company as his assistant. And because of that reason, I didn't want to go out with you in case it might have affected my application."

"Oh!" He felt like a fool now that he knew the real reason she'd wanted him to come back in two weeks. "Well, they should have hired you. Instead of they hired some uppity woman who keeps trying to get me to ask her out whenever I visit my father."

Christa had to cover her mouth with her hand to hide her smile. "Thank you for saying that, but I'm happy with the way things turned out. Martin's Media is paying me more than your father company was offering."

"That doesn't surprise me, as my father is a cheap SOB."

"Harrison, that's an awful thing to say about your father."

"Wait until you meet him, then you'll know there're worst words that better describe him."

For their first date, Harrison took her to Applebee's, and they both ordered steaks. Harrison ordered a beer, but Christa requested a nonalcoholic drink, as she wanted to keep her wits about her while she was with this man.

As they waited for their meal, curious why he'd asked her out, instead of Dana, she inquired about it. "Why haven't you ever asked Dana out?"

Harrison smiled at her question. "Dana and I go way back."

"Really, she never indicated that you two knew each other."

"We went all through school together. She wasn't ever interested in me until my father's company hit it big, then suddenly; she's trying to get my attention. Dana is looking for a rich man to take care of her, while I'm looking for the woman of my dreams so we can live happily ever after," he said, giving her a looked that said he'd found that woman.

His statement stunned her, as the thought of being his wife caused her heart to start pounding in her chest. So jittery at that thought of being married to him for the rest of her life, she had a hard time swallowing the rest of her meal.

That was the first date of many for the two, and before Christa knew what was happening, she'd fallen in love with Harrison Ashby. She still hadn't met his father, but she didn't mind, as she'd learn enough about the man through people at her job who had once worked for him to know she wasn't missing much.

Four weeks after their first date, Harrison took her back to his apartment where a romantic meal was set up. When they finished their candle light dinner, Harrison took hold of her hand, stood and pulled her up into his arms. Then looking deeply into her eyes, he popped the question. "Christa, will you marry me, as I can't live another day without you being my wife."

She gasped as she was stunned by his proposal. "Are you sure you want to marry me?"

He laughed at her question. "I've known that I wanted to marry you from the first second I laid my eyes on you."

His words brought tears to her eyes.

"Sweetheart, don't cry," he said, wiping her tears away with a cloth.

"I can't help it; your words are so romantic."

"So does that mean you'll marry me," he teased.

"Yes, Harrison, I'll marry you."

"I want to get married as soon as possible," Harrison said as he tightened his arms around her.

"Oh, Harrison, I'm ready whenever you are," she replied as he kissed her neck. "Have you talked to your father about us getting married?"

"We aren't speaking at the moment."

Christa wasn't surprised, as father and son always seemed to be at odds with each other about one thing or another. "What was it this time?"

"The same thing as the last time, he's still insisting I quit my job so I can work for him."

"Have you explained to him why you can't do that?" she asked, as she knew he loved being a police detective.

"Many times, but he doesn't want to hear it. I can't tell you much about the case I'm working on right now, but it's very important that I complete my present project. I couldn't quit now even if I wanted to as too many people are depending on me."

Christa knew more about his project than he thought she did, as some of her co-workers had been talking about Judge James who'd been accused of taking bribes in exchange of changing the verdict of some high-profile citizens. She knew that Harrison was building a case against him and once it was done, he would then turn it over the authorities so they could send the man to prison. She told him she was worried about him making a lot of enemies, but he told her that was part of the job.

"Now, let's go tell your family our news."

Christa's family was ecstatic, and welcomed Harrison into the family.

The wedding was a small one, with only Christa's family, Chris and Albert in attendance. It was kept quiet, as Harrison didn't want his father to know anything about his life or his bride.

When Harrison learned of Christa's desire for a baby, he started working diligently on the project, and before long, his hard work had paid off, as Christa was pregnant. She was so excited about the baby, but before she got a chance to tell her family, one of her love ones was murdered.

CHAPTER FIVE

Three months after their secret wedding, Jayna had some news of her own, and couldn't wait for her husband to come home from work so she could tell him. When she saw him driving into the driveway of his apartment complex, she rushed out to meet him.

"Monroe," Jayna cried as she rushed towards him.

"What's wrong?" he asked, concerned why she was at his apartment, as she was still living with Albert.

"Not one thing," she said, putting her hands on either side of his face.

"Then why do your eyes look as if you're going to cry."

"We're pregnant."

Monroe kissed her, then picked her up and spun her around. "Now I'm really going to have to marry you," he teased.

"It's time for you to tell your mother that we're already married."

"Nope."

"Monroe, I'm three months along, if you don't tell her the truth, she'll assume we had premarital sex."

"Jayna, I don't care what my mother thinks."

"Well I do. Besides, I'm tired of sneaking around like two naughty teenagers. I want to sleep with you every night in our bed, in our home. Please tell her, as she already thinks badly of me."

"Honey, I've told you that it isn't you she's upset with, it's the fact I'm not marrying a daughter of one of her friends."

She gave him a hurt look.

"Okay, I tell you what, tonight before the engagement party, I'll tell her that we're already married and then the party can be changed to a wedding celebration instead."

Jayna was thrilled by her husband's words and threw her arms around his neck. "I can hardly wait to see your mother's face when you tell her."

"Do we have time for a little private celebrating before we have to be at the hotel?" he asked, as he nibbled on her ear.

"Not really. But who cares as they can't start the party without us," she replied, as she moved out of his arms, took hold of his hand and started them towards their apartment.

Later as they lay in bed, Jayna put her head on Monroe's shoulder and he began playing with her hair. "What are you thinking about?"

"Now that's you're pregnant, what are you going to do about your job?"

Jayna had only been working at the nearby hospital for the past three months. She enjoyed her job, but she didn't want to be a working mother of a newborn. "I want to quit and stay home with the baby."

Monroe smiled. "I think that would be a good idea."

***

Because of the traffic, Perry arrived twenty minutes later than he'd been told to show up. Afraid he was too late to do the job; he grabbed his rifle bag, hurried into the empty building and ran up the stairs.

By the time he reached the roof, he was out of breath and it took him several seconds before he quit huffing and puffing from climbing the stairs so quickly.

By the time he'd caught his breath, he was at the edge of the roof. Once there, he looked over the side of the building to across the street. Seeing Olivia standing there, he knew he hadn't missed his chance. He then took his rife out of its case and mounted the scope to it, as he wanted to make sure he didn't miss his target. Once that was done, he positioned his gun on the ledge, then knelt down and moved his right eye to the scope. He moved the rifle until he found the front door of the hotel. Now all he had to do was wait for his prey to arrive, do the job he was hired to do, then get the hell out of here without getting caught by the police.

***

Colin had told Monroe he would be at his engagement party, so here he was. He asked his mother to come with him to the party, but she refused, saying if she got close enough to Olivia, she was liable to strike the woman. That and if she got near his father, she was might to throw her arms around and run off to one of the hotel rooms with him. Colin laughed at her comment, as he would have enjoyed seeing her do both of the stated actions.

Colin was walking towards the doors of the hotel, but when he saw Olivia and his father standing in front of the building waiting for Monroe and Jayna to join them, he stopped in his tracks. Afraid Olivia might see him; he took a step back out of the way, and then laughed at his actions, as she didn't even know he existed.

Of course, if he stood next to Colin and their father, Olivia would see how much he looked like them, and would be curious of how they were related. Because of that, he decided to wait where he was until Olivia went inside the building.

He kept his eyes on her, to make sure she didn't look his way and when he saw Olivia scanning the rooftops, he was confused at what she was searching for up there. When she stopped and smiled, he turned his head to see what had caught her attention, but other than seeing the sun glaring off a piece of metal, he didn't see anything interesting up there.

When he saw Monroe's car pulling up, his attention shifted to his brother and his wife. How he wished he could be a fly on the wall when his brother told Olivia that they were already married.

As he continued to watch, Monroe got out and handed his car keys to the attendant. With a happy grin on his face, he started around the front of the car. Once at Jayna's door, he opened the door and took hold of her hand to help her out.

When they reached Olivia and their father, Jayna turned so Colin could see her face. When Colin saw her for the first time since they were teenagers, he sighed, as she was so much more beautiful than she had been all those years ago. His first thoughts were that he wished Monroe wasn't in Jayna's life so he could have her, but no sooner had he contemplated the idea of having her all to himself, he quickly regretted his thoughts.

***

Olivia scanned the rooftops to see if she could find any sign of Perry, when she saw a flash in the sunlight, she glanced to the nearby building's rooftop. When she saw what she was searching for, she held her breath as she watched the barrel of Perry's rifle move into position.

She smiled at knowing her son's engagement would never be announced, and once Jayna was dead; there wouldn't be a need to mention her name ever again. She quickly looked around to see if anyone else had seen it, but all eyes were on Monroe and Jayna as they had just arrived, all that is except Colin. Since Olivia wasn't aware of the man or what he seen seconds before the gunfire, she relaxed.

But even a good thought out plans have a way of not going as intended, for just as Perry pulled the trigger to put a bullet in Jayna's forehead, she sneezed hard. The force of the sneeze was so intense that it caused her body to move downwards, leaving Monroe's chest open. The bullet meant for Jayna, then hit him smack in the chest, just above his heart.

***

When Jayna heard the shot, she assumed it was a car back firing and it wasn't until Monroe knocked into her that she realized something was wrong. She reached out to prevent him from falling, but the weight of his body brought them both down hard onto the pavement. Even as they reached the concrete,

Jayna was unaware that her husband, the father of her baby had been shot.

When she saw the blood on Monroe's chest, she screamed as she realized that the sound she'd heard earlier hadn't been a car back firing, but a gun shot. She quickly put her hand on his chest to stop the blood from pouring out of his body, but it was useless, as the man she loved couldn't be saved.

"Jayna, I love you," Monroe said so softly she barely heard him.

"Monroe, don't you dare leave me," she screamed.

When his blank eyes looked back at her, she knew he was gone, and screamed out a cry of anguish. When someone put their hands on her to move her away from Monroe, she fought them, but Chris was stronger and soon had her in his arms.

***

Chris was stunned by what had just happened, but he had to remain strong for the woman his son had loved. Not caring about her bloody hands, Chris pulled her up into his arms. "Jayna, it's too late, he's gone," he said softly.

As he stood there rubbing her back, hoping to bring her at least some comfort, he looked up and saw Colin in the crowd. Unable to go to him, he let his son know that he's seen him and would talk to him later.

When Christa, her husband, and Grayson appeared at their side, Chris let loose of Jayna, so her family could take care of her. As he stepped away, he looked over at his wife and was stunned to see an evil gaze on her face.

At her expression, he was positive that Olivia was involved somehow with this incident, and because of a simply sneeze, the wrong person had died. If that was true, he knew she would retaliate against Jayna for not being the one to die and he must warn her.

***

Colin heard Jayna sneeze and when the sound of a gunshot filled the air, he watched in horror as Monroe grabbed his chest, fall against Jayna and then went down to the pavement. When he realized his brother had been killed, Colin was in a daze of what had just transpired. Had he somehow caused Monroe's attack by his desire to have Jayna in his life? Then he just as quickly shook his head, as he hadn't killed his brother, faith had.

When Colin felt the tears on his face, he knew it was time for him to leave. He wanted to go to Monroe, but with Olivia there, he couldn't risk her noticing how upset he was at her son's death. He saw his father look up and saw him standing nearby, Colin mouthed that he would call him later.

***

Even though Olivia had been expecting it, she still jumped when she heard the report of the gunshot. Her eyes were on Jayna as she wanted to see her die, but instead she looked on in horror as blood began pouring out of her precious son's chest. She prayed he wasn't seriously injured, but when he took his last breath, she knew that wasn't so.

"No," she screamed, paralyzed in terror at knowing her son was dead because of Jayna's sneeze. She wasn't mad at Perry, as he wasn't to be blamed at killing the wrong person; it was all Jayna's fault. If it weren't for that woman who wanted to marry her son, Monroe would be alive right now. She would get her revenge on Jayna if it was the last thing she did, as she had to pay for her son's death.

Jayna had to die for trying to steal her son from her, but at the thought of another misplaced shot, Olivia decided she would have to be the one to end Jayna's life. The thought brought an evil grin to her face.

"Olivia," Chris called as he touched her arm.

She was so engross with her thoughts of killing Jayna, she hadn't heard Chris calling her name. "What?" she asked as she looked at her husband. Seeing him watching her, her eyes quickly lost the strange glow to them.

"There isn't any more we can do here. Let me take you home."

On the trip home, the car was quiet, both stunned at the thought of losing their son. While Olivia was scheming Jayna's death, Chris was mentally packing his belongings. The divorce papers had been ready for weeks, but he was waiting for after Monroe's wedding before proceeding to tell Olivia he was leaving her.

They hadn't shared the same bedroom since that awful night of Olivia's trickery, but out of respect for his son, he would wait until after Monroe's funeral to move out. Sad but true, the only good thing to come out of his son's death was *now* he could end his marriage without any retaliation from Olivia. Once his marriage was over and done with, he was going to marry the woman he loved.

***

When Perry saw Monroe's body dropping to the pavement, he knew his life was over, so he grabbed the rifle and the bag, then quickly rushed down the steps and out to his car. After he threw the two items into the trunk, he got into his car, and rushed home. When he reached his apartment, he ran inside and threw some of his belongings into a suitcase. He quickly zipped it shut, and then hasty made his way to his car. Once in his car, he pealed out into the street, hightailing it out of town.

When he spotted the police car parked along the street, he started getting nervous, which caused him to want to speed, but he forced himself to keep the car at the posted speed limit. Unbeknown to Perry, just as he passed Officer Bennett's police vehicle, the police officer saw a truck run a red light up ahead, he immediately turned on his lights and sirens to give chase so he could pull over the truck to give him a ticket.

Hearing the siren, Perry assumed the officer was after him, so he quickly increased his speed. Soon he was going so fast that he ran the next light, almost causing an accident. Of course, the officer seeing Perry's chaotic driving, he decided to go after him instead of the truck and a new chase was on.

Parry wasn't worried the officer was going to, caught up with him, as all he had to do was cross the railroad tracks, travel another mile and then he would be at the highway. Once he reached I-70, he would head west towards Kansas, leaving this town and the police officer far behind him.

Perry began to panic when he saw the wooden gate in front of the railroad tracks begin to lower. He looked first to the right, and not seeing a train, he quickly turned towards the left. Seeing the train heading towards him, he figured if he timed it just right, he could pass over the track just before the train, thus preventing the cop car from following.

He kept looking back and forth from the train to the distance he still had to go and was positive he could make it. But in order to fulfill his plan for his escape, he would have to crash through the wooden gate.

As the distance between them rapidly grew smaller, he realized the train was going faster than he'd figured. Afraid he wasn't going to make it, he slammed his foot down on the gas pedal. It was going to be close, but he was sure he could do it.

Seeing what was about to happen, the police officer quickly called into dispatch and requested help, as he was very doubtful the man would be successful in his attempt to beat the train.

The train conductor seeing what the driver of the car was about to do, started blowing his horn, while at the same time, trying to slow down, but it didn't do much good.

As Perry slammed through the barrier, he let out a shout of success that he had made it, and as he did so, his foot lighten up the accelerator just a bit, causing the car to slow down enough that the train hit the back end of it instead of missing him completely.

The force of the impact spun Perry's car around with so much force, that the car was propelled into the side of the still moving train, which quickly demolished the front in of Perry's car, killing him instantly.

The officer stopped near the destroyed barrier, and as he sat there watching the train pass, he could see between the moving train cars that by the inferno coming from the car, that there wouldn't be any survivors. Once the train had passed, Officer Bennett hurried over to the car on foot, and sure enough, he could see the body of a dead man in the car.

Since Officer Bennett's quick thinking had already contacted help, the fire truck arrived on the scene just seconds after the car's impact with the train. They began spraying water onto the fire, quickly extinguishing the flames, preventing the fire from destroying the entire car.

When the investigators appeared, the car was thoroughly searched, and when the trunk was popped open, they were stunned to see the high power rifle with a scope in it. Since everyone working on the scene was aware of the shooting at a local hotel, the rife was quickly processed to see if it had been involved in the incident.

No one was surprised that bullet that had killed Monroe Regan had come from the rifle that was retrieved at the scene of the car wreck. What was puzzling was why had this two-bit hoodlum killed the young man? Some speculated that it was a hit job, but if so, who had hired the killer and why did someone want Monroe Regan dead.

When Jayna was taken to the police station for questioning regarding the shooting, Harrison went with his sister-in-law for support, telling his fellow coworkers that she wasn't involved in her husband's death and that they needed to look elsewhere.

Since Chris had spoken to Harrison about his suspicions concerning his wife involvement in the shooting, they picked up Olivia and brought her down to the station. Nothing was determined by her interrogation, other than she seemed saddened by the news of Parry's horrible death. The officers continued to try to find a link between her and the shooter, as they were sure Olivia was somehow mix up in the incident, as she was the only one that had a motive.

When Jayna learned that the police concluded that she had been the intended victim, she was greatly upset to think it was her fault that her husband had been killed.

***

When Jayna and Monroe told the family that they were planning on living at the ranch after the wedding, Grayson had moved back to his family home, taking all their animals with him. Albert not wanting to intrude on Monroe and Jayna's marriage decided to move into an apartment in a retirement center so the newlyweds could have the house all to themselves after their wedding.

But before Albert could do anything about moving into the retirement center, Monroe had been killed. Unsure what to do now about his living situation, Albert decided to wait and see what Jayna did before he made a final decision.

Since Jayna thought Albert wanted to move, she told Albert that she planned to live in Monroe's apartment, and started moving some of her belongings to her new home.

Albert decided before he put the place up for sale, he would ask Colin if he wanted the ranch, and if he didn't want it, *then* he would put it up for sale and move into an apartment.

Colin knew he'd been his Great Grandfather's second choice, in owning his land, but it didn't matter to him, as he'd always dreamed of living here in the family home. So he told Albert that he wanted the place, but only if he would continue to live in his home with him.

His dream was that someday after Jayna had time to mourn the loss of her husband, he would ask her out. Maybe if he was lucky, someday she would be his wife.

CHAPTER SIX

Even though Jayna proved she and Monroe had been married, Olivia still cut her completely out of the loop of the plans for Monroe's funeral. Then to get back at Jayna, Olivia bought a single plot for Monroe, which rested between two family plots, so Jayna wouldn't be able to have her internal rest next to Monroe.

When Jayna found out where Monroe was to be buried, she called Chris crying to tell him about what Olivia had done. Chris was appalled of Olivia's actions, and assured Jayna that on the day of the funeral, her husband would be buried in a location that would have a place for her next to him.

The day before the funeral, with her sister by her side, Jayna had her first ultra sound and learned that she was having a baby boy. She and Monroe had already picked out baby names, and so her son's name would be Preston Albert Regan.

The funeral was extremely hard on Jayna, as the tension in the room from Olivia's hatred of her was overwhelming and if it weren't for Chris and her family, she wouldn't have made it through the ordeal.

She had survived the service without breaking down, but when they moved to the gravesite, and she saw his casket resting over his final resting place, she started sobbing. She wished she'd die so she could be with her husband, but since she had their child to think of, she had to accept the fact that she had to live on without the man she loved.

Chris put his arm around her. "I wish I could make this easier for you. If you should ever need anything, anything at all, just call, and I'll come a running."

"I'm going to have Monroe's baby," she whispered softly in his ear, hoping Olivia who was sitting next to Chris didn't hear her.

Her words brought a small smile to his face. When some guests walked over to Olivia, Chris stood, took hold of Jayna's hand, and stepped away so they could talk privately.

"How am I going to raise a baby without my husband?"

"I'll be there for you no matter what," Chris said, wondering how this circumstance would affect him leaving Olivia. "If you need any money or even a ride the doctor's office, you call me."

"Thank you."

"Did Monroe know about the baby?"

"Yes, he was so excited. We were going to tell everyone the night he was killed that we were already married and was going to be parents in six months."

Chris looked around for his wife to be sure she wasn't around to overhear their conversation. "When do you want to tell Olivia about the baby?" he asked.

"I can't do it." She looked at him with the sadness pair of eyes. "I was wondering if you would do it for me."

"Yes, I can do that for you. I'll tell her after we get home," he said, already dreading the conversation, for knowing his wife, there was bound to be a scene.

"My sonogram showed we were having a baby boy. Monroe wanted to name him Preston Albert, if that's okay with you."

He smiled, as he was touched his grandson would have his middle name. "I'm honored."

***

When they had moved to the gravesite, Olivia was angered by the fact that when they sat down, Jayna had sat next to Chris. Even though she'd proven she and Monroe had been married for three months, Olivia didn't think the girl had the right to sit on the front row. Not only that, but Chris gave Jayna more attention, than he did her. Didn't Chris care that she was grieving too?

Olivia's mind busy on Jayna and her hatred for her, didn't even realized her son wasn't going to be buried in the spot she'd chose, as the green mat on the ground covered the empty burial plots around them. It was a good thing, because if she'd known she would have caused an awful scene during the service, something she was well known for among the family. And with life's many unexpected turns, Olivia wouldn't ever learn about the change in burial plots.

***

After the service, Chris let Jayna's family take her away. As he turned to go back to Olivia, he saw Elena and their son standing nearby. He couldn't speak with either of them now without his wife becoming suspicious, so he nodded slightly to acknowledge their presents, and then he moved to his wife's side. "Let's go home."

Dreading the thought of telling Olivia about Jayna's pregnancy, the car ride home was a quiet one, same as the one to the funeral home had been. After Chris pulled into the garage, he got out of the car, and headed into the house without saying a word.

He opened the door and went inside, heading straight for the liquor cabinet in the family room. After pouring a double of whisky, he downed half of it with one swallow.

"Did that help?" Olivia asked sarcastically from the door.

He looked over at his wife as she entered the room. "Too soon to tell. Sit down Olivia; I have something to tell you."

"Do I get a drink first?"

"Go ahead," he said, not even bothering to offer to make it for her.

Olivia was a bit stunned by his comment, as he usually fixed her drink without even asking. As she looked at his expression, she knew he had something important to say. Since their son was dead, she didn't have to guess what it was about, so she fixed a double martini, and then went to sit across from him.

"Okay, what is it you have to say."

He wanted to tell her he was leaving her, but decided to hold off until after he knew how she was going to take his news about Jayna before telling her about the divorce. "Jayna is pregnant."

Olivia was stunned at first by her husband's statement, but then she began to glow as a wicked plot began forming in her mind. She was going to sue for custody of Monroe's child, as what better revenge on Jayna than taking the child from her and raising her grandchild as her own.

As soon as she was alone, she would call her lawyer, Walt Utt and have him start the proceeding of getting custody of Monroe's child. Chris better not get in her way, because if he tried to interfere in her plans, she would hire someone to kill him too.

Chris wasn't shock when Olivia's eyes seemed to glisten, as he assumed she'd come up with some evil plan to hurt Jayna. "Do you want to tell me what you're planning?"

Olivia quickly changed her expression. "Planning? I wasn't planning anything. I'm just happy to know we're going to be grandparents."

Now that he knew for sure she was up to something fiendish, he realized the announcement he was leaving her would have to wait. Knowing he had to get away from her before he said something he regretted, he started for the door. "I'm going to my room."

Olivia wanted to stop him and have him put his arms around her to comfort her, but then she shook her head. She'd lost that right the night she'd doped him up and taken advantage of him in the hope of making their marriage legal. She should feel bad for that incident, but then she wouldn't have had Monroe in her life.

***

Grayson drove his sister to her new apartment, and when they arrived, he walked her to the door. "Would you like me to come in for a while?"

Jayna smiled at her brother. "Thanks, but I would like to be alone."

"If you need anything, just call me and I'll come a running."

"I think I'll lie down and rest for a while."

"Christa and I'll come over tomorrow and help you get settled in the apartment."

"Grayson, thank you."

He kissed her good-bye, then left.

Jayna watched until Grayson got into his truck before she closed apartment door. She had a lot of things to do around the apartment, but instead, she went to the bedroom, removed her dress, and lay down on the bed. The thought of living here without Monroe tore at her heart, and she began crying. Exhausted from the day and all the tears she'd shed, she was soon asleep.

***

When the ringing phone woke Jayna, she was confused for a moment of where she was. As her mind cleared, she realized she was sleeping in Monroe's bed. The phone rang again before she could reach for it. "Hello?"

"Mrs. Jayna Regan?"

"Yes, this is she."

"My name is Walt Utt; I'm Olivia Regan's lawyer."

Jayna had a terrible feeling she wasn't going to like what he had to say. "How may I help you?"

"I'm calling as a courtesy to you to inform you that Mrs. Regan is suing for custody of your child. To save time and legal fees from hashing all this out in court, I have a paper for you to sign that will relinquish all your legal rights to your son."

Jayna was shocked by his statement. "Is this some sort of joke?"

"No, madam. You should be receiving the form in the mail tomorrow. Just sign it and sent it back in the address stamped envelope."

"I would thank you for calling, but since I would be lying, I won't." She simply hung up the phone without saying another word. So traumatize by the call, she simply sat down on the floor and began crying.

***

Jayna had prayed Olivia's lawyer call had been a sick joke, but when she went to get the mail the next morning, she found the letter he mentioned was there waiting for her. When she opened it, she saw the legal paperwork stated that Olivia Regan would receive custody of her son the day she gave birth to him.

If she signed it, not only would she be relinquishing all her rights to her son, she wouldn't ever see the child again. If she didn't sign it, she would have to go to court, where she would have a fight on her hands, a fight she was sure she would lose due to the fact that Olivia Regan's had many legal connections, including the well-known crooked Judge James.

Monroe had told her if for any reason she ever needed a good lawyer to call Colin, as he would take care of her. She hadn't spoken to Colin Sparkman since that summer he came to stay, but Monroe had told her that she could trust him and right now, she hoped that was true. Not sure, what else to do, she called and made an appointment with Colin.

***

When Sally, Colin's assistant was ready to leave for the night, she went into his office to tell him about the new appointment he had tomorrow. "I'm leaving for the night, but I wanted you to know that Jayna Regan has scheduled a meeting with you tomorrow."

Colin was surprised by her announcement, as he couldn't figure out why Jayna had made an appointment to see him. "Is this regarding a personal or business matter?"

Sally frown, as she felt she hadn't done her job properly. "Since she said she needed to make an appointment with you, I assume it's regarding a legal matter. Should I call her back and ask her?"

"No, that's not necessary. What time is the appointment for?"

"Ten. Is there anything else you need to night?"

"No, you go on and I'll see you tomorrow."

After Sally left, Colin couldn't stop wondering why Jayna would want to see him. He thought about calling his father and asking him if he knew why she would need a lawyer, but before he could, the phone rang.

When he looked down at the caller ID, and saw it was his father, he had to laugh. He quickly picked up the phone. "Just the man I was thinking of calling."

"Hello? Who is this and what have you done with my son."

"Very funny. I may not call you as often as Monroe did, but I do call regularly."

"Yes, you do. I was just teasing you."

"Is there a reason you're calling so late in the day?"

"I'm calling for three reasons. The first one is that I wanted you to know that Jayna is pregnant. Second one is when I told Olivia, she seemed especially happy about it for some strange reason."

"You think she's planning something?"

"Yes, but I'm not sure what."

"And the third reason you call?"

"They've matched the bullet that killed Monroe to the gun of the man who was killed in the train collision the night Monroe was killed."

"At least we know justice has been served regarding Monroe's killer."

"Yes, but we don't know why he did it. Something tells me that Olivia may have hired him to kill Jayna, but I don't have any proof of that. Why were you thinking about calling me?"

"I wanted you to know Jayna has made an appointment to see me for tomorrow. Do you think it has something to do with her being pregnant?"

"I would say that's a good guess."

"If it's okay with Jayna, I'll call you tomorrow after her appointment to let you know why she needed to see me."

"I'll be waiting to hear from you."

The two men said good-bye, but Colin couldn't stop wondering why Jayna was coming to see him. Finally, he picked up some files and started through them to keep his mind off her and tomorrow's visit.

CHAPTER SEVEN

When Jayna stepped into Colin's office and saw him for the first time since she was thirteen, she gasped. Not only was he better looking than he'd been all those years ago, but she'd immediately felt an attraction to him, which caused her feel disloyal to her husband's memory.

Other than the fact Monroe had only been gone a few days, she knew there wasn't anything wrong in her attraction to this man. Besides, she was here on business, and that's how she was going to keep it.

"Thank you, Mr. Sparkman for seeing me on such short notice," she said, taking hold of Colin's hand. "It's been a few years since we last saw each other."

When Colin took hold of her hand, a slight tingle of excitement ran up his arm, causing him to feel as if he was in Heaven. How he wished she wasn't his brother's widow, as he would love to ask her to go out to dinner with him. Then he shook his head, as this was a business meeting between a client and a lawyer, not a sexual hook up.

"Yes it has, and please call me, Colin. I'm sorry about Monroe's death. I wanted to give you my condolences at the funeral, but there never seem to be a right time."

She was touched Colin had been there. "Thank you. I'm sorry, I didn't see you there, but if I had, I would have said hello."

"I was there with my mother, as she and Monroe became very close while we were growing up." As soon as the words left his mouth, he realized he'd revealed more than he should. He anxiously waited for her to ask about their relationship, and was relieved when she didn't.

"I'm glad he had someone other than his mother in his life when he was a child." She quickly wiped the few tears that had appeared as she talked about her husband.

"What can I do for you today?"

"Olivia's lawyer contacted me, stating that she wants custody of my baby. When I received a legal document in the mail yesterday, I realized that I needed legal help."

Colin was shocked by her statement, as he didn't think even Olivia would sink so low.

"Monroe told me that I could trust you so that's why I'm here. I was hoping you can help me with this situation."

Colin cringed at her comment, as she may trust him now, but what will happen once she learned the truth about him and his relationship with Monroe. "Monroe was a good man," he said, wondering what else Monroe had said about him, but refrained from asking.

She gave him a weak smile. "Yes, he was. I haven't spoken with Mr. Regan regarding this matter, so I'm not sure of his involvement. Since they're married, I assume he's backing her."

"Don't assume anything until you talk to Mr. Regan personally. Do you mind if I talk to him about your situation with his wife? Maybe he can tell me more about why she's doing this."

"No, you can talk to whoever you think is necessary. I don't have the money to fight Monroe's family in a legal battle. With Mrs. Regan's ties in the community, I'm not sure if there's a judge who would go against her in court."

"I'm sure you're right."

She frowned, as she didn't like the sound of his answer. With Monroe's insurance money, she could run away, but she didn't want to leave her family behind. Even if she did leave the country, there wasn't enough money for her to hide from Olivia forever. Whatever she did, she knew Olivia wouldn't give up until she had her son in her possession.

Colin reached out and took hold of her hand to comfort her. "Why are you frowning? Is something else wrong?"

"Do you think I should leave the country before the baby's born?"

Colin gave her a thoughtful look. "You could, but knowing Olivia, I would be afraid of her attacking your family in the hope of getting you to return to home.

She gasped. "I hadn't even thought about her hurting me through my siblings."

"From what I know of Olivia's determination, since she wants your child, she'll do anything to obtain her goal. How are your brother and sister?" he asked only to be polite, as he already knew the answer to his question.

"Christa is married to Harrison Ashby, and Grayson has recently moved back into our family home. Is there anything you can do to help me with my situation?"

At first, he wasn't sure how to help her, and then a brilliant idea came to him. "I can only think of one option that will guarantee to protect you from her getting your son." If he was going to protect Monroe's widow and their child, he had to act before Olivia was aware that Jayna was even talking to a lawyer about fighting her. He stood, moving around his desk, he sat down in the chair next to her.

Jayna simply stared at him, unsure if what he said was possible. "I give up. What would that be?"

He knew how much Monroe loved the woman in front of him, and so it was up to him to protect his brother's child from Olivia. "You'll have to marry me," he said. As soon as he spoke, he regretted his words, as he shouldn't have just popped out this suggestion, but slowly worked up to it.

He probably should have called his father to talk it over with him before he'd proceeded with this, but it was too late now. So if Jayna agreed to his proposal, he would just surprise his father at the same time they did Olivia. Besides, this way Olivia couldn't accuse his father of knowing about the wedding behind her back.

Not only that, but if his father knew what they were about to do, he may try to talk him out of this and he really did want to marry Jayna. It wasn't because of her unborn child, but because he was in love with her.

Jayna laughed out loud, as she found his comment comical. "I'm sorry, but I don't see how my marrying you is going to protect my son. Wouldn't any man do?"

God no, Colin thought to himself. He needed to tell her about his relationship to Monroe, but was afraid that if he did, she would refuse his offer. "Let's just say, I have my own connections, ones Olivia wouldn't be able to entice to go against me."

Jayna was stunned by his statement. "I'm impressed, and from your tone, I'd say you're pretty sure of the association to be certain of the outcome. Even though I'd like to refuse your offer, I can't take the chance of Monroe's mother winning custody of my baby, so I accept your proposal."

Colin nodded, as he understood, she had accepted his proposal for one reason, and that one reason only.

"If we did get married, how long of a relationship between us are we talking about here?" she asked, not at all prepared for the answer he was going to give her.

"Until all our children graduate high school," he stated with a serious expression.

Her mouth dropped open, as she'd been shaken by his statement. "Children? Who said anything about *children*?"

He laughed at her traumatized expression, and then pushed her mouth closed with his index finger. "I did. If we're to get married, I want to have children of my own as well."

"I can understand that, but don't you want to marry someone you love and have children with them?"

Her question threw him, as he was unsure how to answer it. If he answered it honestly, she would know she was the woman he wanted. So instead, he asked one of his own. "So do you still want to say yes?"

She was confused why he hadn't answered her question. It couldn't be because he had feelings for her, as they hadn't seen each other for almost ten years. "Colin, why do you want to marry me? And I want the truth," she stated firmly.

That was easy for him to answer, as he had more than one reason why he wanted to marry her. "To piss Olivia Regan off."

Jayna started giggling and soon was laughing so hard, tears began running down her cheeks.

"I apologize if I've offended you," he said as he handed her a tissue.

"No, it wasn't that," she said, taking the tissue he offered. "I just wasn't expecting a lawyer to talk that way in front of a client. What did she do to make you dislike her so much?"

"Besides the way she raised Monroe?"

"Yes."

"I hated the way she's treated my father." He knew he was walking on shaking ground by bringing his father into the conversation, but it sort of popped out of his mouth.

Jayna wanted to ask what he meant, but by the tightness of his mouth, she knew it was best to let it go for now. "I'm sorry."

"Me too."

"How soon should we get married?" she asked.

"Immediately."

Since the baby wasn't due for another six months, she expected him to say sometime in the next few months, so his answer flabbergasted her. "Colin, we haven't seen each other since we were teenagers. Shouldn't we sit down and get reacquainted before we plunge into a twenty year commitment."

"No, as I don't want Olivia to know what we're about to do until after we're married. We could fly out to Las Vegas and be married before the day is out."

She shook her head, as she didn't want to get married the same thing way that she and Monroe had done.

Misunderstanding her response, he assumed she was telling him she wouldn't marry him until she knew something about him. "What do you want to know?" he asked. "Do you want to know how much I'm attracted to you? Or that kissing you is all I've thought about since the minute I first saw you when we were teenagers." Before she could answer, he stood and pulled her into his arms.

"Colin," she said while trying to push him away. When he let go of her, she took in a deep breath, hoping to calm the butterflies in her stomach his touch had caused in her. "At least, one can't say you aren't blunt and to the point."

He laughed. "So what do you say about us going to Las Vegas. I think the sooner Olivia knows she isn't going to be getting her hands on your child, the better."

"Put it that way, I would have to agree, but I really don't want to go to Las Vegas"

"Any reason why not?" he asked as he studied her face.

"That's where Monroe and I went to get married. Why don't we just get married somewhere here in town? I'm sure we can tie the knot here without Olivia finding out about it before hand."

Colin felt horrible at his comment about going to Las Vegas. "I'm sorry; I'd forgotten where the two of you were married. How about going to Eureka Springs, Arkansas for the wedding, as then we can spend our honeymoon there as well."

She didn't want to think about having a honeymoon with this man, especially since Monroe hadn't been gone long enough for her to be in another man's bed. "A honeymoon isn't necessary."

"The marriage has to be consummated," he stated, his eyes never leaving hers.

Her eyes widened at his comment. "You want to have sex with me as soon as we get married? I'm not ready for that part of our marriage."

"You can keep your eyes close and pretend I'm Monroe." He groaned as soon as his insensitive words tumbled from his lips.

His comment outraged her to the point she'd slapped his face without even thinking about what she was doing. "That comment is an insult to my husband's memory," she stated, her tears enforcing her words.

Colin felt ghastly for hurting her. "I'm sorry. I don't know why I said it. It wasn't my intent to hurt you or disrespect Monroe's memory."

"I'd like to tell you forget this whole thing, but then Olivia would win and I'd regret it for the rest of my life. I really don't think see how Olivia is going to know whether or not we have sex."

"If Olivia takes you to court and you're under oath, will you be able to lie on the stand if you're asked if the marriage was consummated."

She shook her head. "I don't think so, as I'm not very good at lying."

"So there's your answer."

"I'm sure as two adults, who are attracted to the other; we can make our wedding night a memorable one."

"You're attracted to me?" Colin knew Jayna had loved Monroe, so he silently rejoiced the fact she wasn't indifferent to him as a man, nor had she cancelled their wedding at his rude comment.

Jayna blushed. "I'm not blind. You're a very attractive man, for some reason you even reminded me of Monroe, especially in the eyes and some of your mannerisms," she uttered as she stared at him.

Her comment about him resembling Monroe was the perfect opening to tell her about his relationship with her husband, but the words wouldn't come. "I thought you were marrying me just for the sake of your baby."

"I am," she stated, her eyes remaining on his. She wasn't being honest with him, as she did desire him in a sexual way, but she wasn't about to admit that to him.

"Okay then, how about we seal our bargain with a kiss." He pulled her into his arms before she could response either way. Once he started kissing her, he didn't want to stop. When he felt her pushing at his chest to get out of his arms, his lips moved away from hers, but he didn't release her.

"I think our bargain has been definitely sealed," she said breathlessly. Tears formed in her eyes, as the kiss had excited her more than she thought it should have.

He felt bad for causing her tears. "Sorry, I sort of got carried away. I didn't intend to offend you."

"I want you to know that even though we're getting married and will have to consummate our marriage, I don't want to be intimate again until I've had time to grieve Monroe's death properly." She gave him a look to say she meant there wouldn't be any more kissing of any kind after their wedding night.

Colin nodded, as he had to respect her feeling for his brother. "I'm willing to give you at least two years before we start sharing a bed."

"Thank you, that's more than I could ask for."

"No, it isn't. But I don't know if I could wait any longer than that to have you in my bed every night." His comment caused him to blush, and so he had to clear his throat before he could continue. "Again

I apologize for my thoughtless words. I'll make the arrangement for the wedding to be tomorrow as I don't want to take the chance of Olivia stopping us."

"I would need to go home and pack some clothes." She started getting nervous when he didn't let her go, but continued to gaze into her eyes. "I can't leave until you let go of me."

Reluctantly, he released her and she took several steps back.

"We haven't talked about our living arrangements," he uttered softly.

She frowned, as she hadn't even given any thought of where they would be living once they tied the knot. "I guess we'll have to live together for this marriage scheme to work."

Her words hurt, as he thought of this marriage as more than *some scheme* to protect her son. "Albert has offered me the ranch and I've accepted his offer."

"Really? Why did he do that?" she asked, confused why Albert would do such a thing.

"He thinks of me as family," he responded honestly. "I would like to live out at the ranch if it's okay with you."

She smiled at him, as she was relieved by his suggestion, as she hated living in Monroe's apartment without him being there. "Living at the ranch will be fine. I'll take my old room and you can have the one Grayson was using before he moved back home."

Colin didn't like that arrangement, but knew he couldn't expect they would be sharing the same bed. "You should know that Albert will be living with us," he said, then waited nervously for her response.

"That's good to hear," she replied with a smile.

"Then you don't mind if he stays?"

"No, as he's part of my family too."

Colin smiled at her comment. "Once we're settled, I'll clean out the other bedroom for the baby."

"Thank you."

He simply nodded. "In order for this to work, we have to be able get married before anyone can interfere and prevent the wedding, so I don't want you to tell a single soul what we're about to do."

She gave him a weak smile. "That's just what Monroe said before we tied the knot. You two seem to think alike."

Her words were the perfect opening for him to reveal his relationship with Monroe, but he remained quiet, as he was afraid, she wouldn't marry him if she knew the truth. "Must be all the years we've been together."

"Monroe mentioned you two met when you were just young boys."

"That's right, we were five," he said, leaving it at that. "Let me check the Internet regarding wedding in Eureka Springs."

She was expecting Colin to expand on their relationship, so his change in the subject had thrown her. She started to ask him to elaborate on the subject, but when he turned his back to her and walked over to his computer, she realized it wouldn't do any good to ask.

Colin hurried over to his computer and sat down. He hoped she wouldn't ask him to explain how he and Monroe met, as he would have to lie to her, and there were enough lies between them as it was.

He clicked on the Internet icon to look up a hotel in Eureka Springs that held weddings. Once he had their number, he called them and said he needed to make a reservation for a wedding, and he needed it as soon as possible.

When the woman said that they had a cancellation for the one o'clock slot for the next afternoon, he took it. It was perfect, as it gave them plenty of time to drive down there tomorrow so they could complete their objective before anyone knew what they were getting married.

Once he knew their schedule, he told her to go home and pack a bag. He wanted her to get plenty of rest, as tomorrow would be a busy day for them, as the trip to Eureka Springs would take them at least five hours by car. After they arrived, they would have the wedding, see some of the sights, and then have their wedding night, and the next morning, they would return home. They would go their separate way for now, but after tomorrow, they would be a couple in all sense of the word. He kept expecting her to change her mind about marrying him, but she never did.

After Jayna left, Colin called his father.

"So why did Jayna come see you?"

"You aren't going believe this, but Olivia wants custody of Monroe and Jayna's baby."

Chris let out a vulgar exclamation. "It's going to have to be up to you to save Preston from having Olivia as his mother."

"I'm working on it."

"What do you plan to do?"

"I'm not at liberty to say, but you'll be one of the first persons to know."

"Is it legal?" Chris asked him quietly.

Colin laughed. "Of course, it's legal and hopefully it will work to our benefit."

"I hope you're right. I'm glad you took your great grandpa up on his offer."

"I told him that the only way I would move out to the ranch was if he stayed, as it will always be his home."

"He's thrilled, as he wasn't ready to leave his home."

They said good-bye, and then Colin went home to pack his suitcase.

After he took his suitcase and set it by his front door, he went to the kitchen to get a cold beer. As he sat there slowly consuming his beverage, he wondered if Jayna would ever accept him as her true husband. Would they be able to make their marriage work, raising Preston along-side of any children they had together? Only time would tell if this scheme of his would work out to his liking.

CHAPTER EIGHT

As she left Colin's office, Jayna thought about wearing the dress she'd wore when she married Monroe, but she couldn't do it. Not having another dress appropriate for a wedding at home, she decided to stop at the local bridal shop to find a dress for her second wedding.

She was worried she wouldn't find a dress that wasn't a bridal gown, but she was in luck as someone had returned a *Mother of the Bride* outfit that was perfect for this occasion, not too dressy, but formal enough to wear for her wedding.

The whole time Jayna packed her suitcase for the trip, she tried to keep her mind off her wedding night, as the thought of sleeping with Colin made her queasy.

She really didn't know the man, and not only that, but she felt disloyal to Monroe's memory to be thinking of having sex with another man so soon after his death.

Once in bed, she closed her eyes and waited for sleep to come, but she just laid there thinking about what she was about to do with Colin. Now that she accepted his marriage proposal, she was worried. If this ploy weren't successful, she would be married to a man, she didn't really know any more.

After she tossed and turned for over an hour, she gave up being able to fall asleep on her own, went to the bathroom, and took one of her sleeping pills. As she laid there waiting for the pill to work, she kept her mind off Colin and their wedding, and ten minutes later, she was asleep.

***

When she woke up the next morning and saw how late it was, she jumped out of bed and ran to take her shower. After drying her hair, she'd pinned her hair up in a lose bun. Next, she put on her make-up, and when she was satisfied with her appearance, it was time to get dressed.

She put on the skirt first, and then added a soft blue blouse that matched the blue in the skirt. After putting on the jacket that went with the outfit, she moved to the mirror to look at herself.

As she stared at the person looking back at her, she wondered if she was doing the right thing. As she stood there staring at her reflection, tears appeared as she wondered if Monroe would approve of what she was about to do. She knew Monroe had thought highly of Colin, but what would her husband think if he knew she was marrying this man. Would he understand why she was doing this?

She shook her head, thinking he must be turning over in his grave at knowing she was getting married just days of his death. With that thought, she came to the decision she couldn't marry Colin and have sex with him as if Monroe had never been in her life. Instead, she was going to take the insurance money and run away to a foreign country until her son turned eighteen.

So when her doorbell rang, she just stood there, too scared to let the man into her apartment that she promised to marry and tell him she changed her mind. She wondered if she didn't answer, he would take the hint and leave without her having to tell him she wasn't going to marry him.

When that someone started pounding hard on the door, she realized she had to let him in and tell him to his face she wasn't going to marry him. She had just opened the door when her phone began ringing. "Excuse me, Colin."

Colin stepped into the apartment, closing the door behind him. As he watched her go to the phone, he wondered about the expression he'd seen on her face when she'd opened the door to him. Was she planning on telling him the wedding was off? God, he hoped not.

"Hello?" she answered absent-mindedly, as her mind was on telling Colin she was cancelling their wedding.

"Jayna, I'm calling to see when I can pick up the paperwork regarding your relinquishing custody of your baby," a cold voice asked.

"Olivia," she squeaked. Her petrified eyes quickly flew over at Colin, unsure how to reply.

Colin came over and took hold of her hand, mouthing to her that he wanted to know what she wanted.

After she pointed to the paperwork lying on her desk, Colin went over to the desk and picked it up. "Tell her you're mailing it now," he whispered in her ear.

"I was just about to put the paperwork into the mail," she muttered into the phone.

"Don't bother. I'll have someone come over to get it from you."

"No, it isn't any bother. Besides I'm just about to step out the door," she said quickly, hoping she had said the right thing. She looked over at him and when Colin nodded his head, she was relieved.

"Where are you going, dear," she asked in her usual demeaning tone.

Jayna smiled. "That madam isn't any of your damn business," she said bravely, then promptly hung up the phone. She turned to Colin, her previous decision not to marry him altered. "I'm ready to leave."

Colin eyed her for a moment. "Are you sure you want to go through with this?"

"I'm not sure about anything except that my mother-in-law is probably on her way to my apartment as we speak. By her phone call, I realize she isn't going to stop looking for me until she has my son in her possession. When should I tell her that I'm not giving up my son?"

"Tear up the form and mail it back to her, she'll get the hint." He decided if she did as he suggested, it meant she was going to go ahead with their plans for them to marry. If she didn't, then he'd understand she'd changed her mind.

She took the paperwork from him, then proceeded to rip in up into small pieces. When he handed her the preaddressed envelope they'd left with her, she dropped the shredded paper into it, and then quickly licked the seal. Just as she smiled at him, the phone rang, causing her to jump. She quickly looked over at the phone, back at him and then to the phone again.

Colin took hold of her suitcase that was sitting by the door, opened her apartment door, and put out his hand to her. "If you're ready, let's get out of here before they arrive and start pounding at your door."

She was relieved he hadn't asked her why she'd looked the way she had when she'd answered the door. But then maybe he knew she had been going to refuse his marriage offer, that is, until Olivia's phone call. As they passed the apartment mail slot, she pushed the envelope in, and then continued on her way.

***

Even though it was a five-hour drive to Eureka Springs, Jayna was quiet during most of the trip. She was accepting what they were about to do, as she came to realize marrying Colin was the only way for her to keep her son once he was born. She sensed Colin's eyes on her several times during the drive there, but he too remained quiet.

When they stopped about two and a half hours later at a gas station, he'd turned off the engine and then twisted to face her. "We could come up with another plan if you rather not marry me."

Jayna smiled as she turned to look at him. "Colin, it isn't you. It's that I feel as if I'm being disloyal to my husband's memory by marrying so soon after his death. Not only that, you and I are practically strangers since it's been so long since we've seen each other."

Colin took hold of her hand. "I understand what you're saying. Instead of marrying for love, we're doing it because of special circumstances, so you can protect your son."

"I know, but I can't help feeling somehow this is wrong. What will my family think of me when they learned I married a man I haven't seen since I was a teenager?"

"So what do you want to do? Get married or run away to some foreign country where you don't even speak the language?"

She gave him a weak smile. "Neither."

"I don't mean to rush you, but we're running out of time here."

"My mother in-law isn't giving me any choice. I just wished I knew if my father-in-law was on her side or mine."

"I can answer that one, as Chris Regan wouldn't ever steal someone's child in order to replace one of his own."

She looked at him, unsure how well he knew Monroe's father. "You sound so sure of that."

"I've known him all my life and I greatly admire the man."

Jayna started to ask how that was possible since he didn't meet Monroe until they were five, but then she decided he must have met Mr. Regan before he'd met Monroe. "Yes, but he's married to her."

"When I told him what Olivia was trying to pull, he told me it was up to me to protect your son from Olivia, and that's what I'm doing by marrying you."

Jayna could only hope Colin was telling her the truth about what her father-in-law had said to him, as she couldn't afford to have Chris to be on Olivia's side of this custody battle.

***

Finally, they arrived at the hotel. While Colin went to check them in, Jayna looked around her surrounding, watching and waiting for her mother-in-law to show up to stop them from getting married.

Colin looked over at her. "It's going to be okay. Your mother-in-law hasn't any way of knowing what we're about to do."

Jayna gave him a frail smile. "I hope you're right," she replied nervously.

He studied her expression, searching for some sort of idea what was going through her mind. "You haven't said anything to anyone have you?"

She shook her head. "No, I didn't even tell Christa or Grayson that I was leaving the city."

He took hold of her hand and gave it a light squeeze. “That must have been hard for you to do.”

“Yes, it was. I have always been able to tell my twin sister everything,” she replied tearfully.

“You can explain it to them when you get home.”

She let out a hysterical laugh. “How can I explain to my family about marrying another man just days after losing my husband without both of them thinking badly of me?”

“I assume they know how your mother-in-law is. Explain this was the only way to protect your child from her.”

“I just hope they understand why I felt I had no other choice but to marry you.”

***

During their wedding service, Jayna keep expecting Olivia Regan to run into the room and scream, *Stop or I’ll shoot* a line from an old movie she’d seen with Monroe shortly before his death. When the minister said they were man and wife, Jayna sighed heavily, causing Colin to look over at her.

He sure hoped she didn't regret marrying him, as now that she was his wife, he wasn't going to let her go without a fight.

"Mr. Sparkman, you may kiss your bride."

Colin wasn't sure if Jayna would let him kiss her, but knew it was something he had to do. He gently took hold of each of her arms, then leaned over and kissed her. Just as he began to deepen his kiss, he felt her pinching his stomach and he quickly took a step back.

"I'm sorry," he whispered faintly so the minister wouldn't hear.

"It's okay. I understand."

After they signed all the paperwork, there wasn't anything left to do except to thank the minister.

"Thank you."

"Good luck to you both."

Jayna smiled at him. "Thank you. It was a beautiful service."

The truth of it was this ceremony had been a lot more beautiful than the one she'd had with Monroe in Las Vegas. There they'd been just one of many getting married that day, but today; it had just been the two of them.

When she turned back to Colin, he took hold of her hand, and they left the minister's home.

"Are you ready to eat some lunch?"

"I'm hungry, but not sure if I'll be able to keep it down."

"Is the baby causing you some distress?" he asked looking at belly.

"No, just stress from everything that has happened today."

"I'm sorry Jayna. If I thought there was another option, I would have suggested it." Of course, he refrained from mentioning that he hadn't even tried to think of another solution to her problem.

She reached over and touched his arm. "I know. I really appreciate all you have done for me. Not many lawyers would have gone to the extreme you have in order to protect my unborn child."

"I'm doing this for Monroe as well. I'm just glad he didn't marry some buck tooth, one eye, bleach blond barracuda."

Jayna laughed. "What a sweet thing to say," she teased.

Colin stopped at a local café for lunch, and after looking over the menu, he ordered a steak. Jayna deciding she needed to eat at least something ordered soup and a turkey sandwich. There wasn't much talking as they waited for their food, as they were both thinking about what would happen when they returned to the room.

She thought she would be relieved when the waiter brought their meals, but once it came, she realized when they finished eating; they would go back to the hotel.

Seeing she was just eyeing her soup instead of eating in, he reached over and took hold of her hand. "Are you okay?"

"I'm just a bit nervous about what we're going to do tonight," she said, keeping her eyes on her food.

"I know you shouldn't been consuming any alcohol, but maybe drinking something might help relax you a bit. Do you think one glass of wine would hurt?"

"Probably not. Colin, are you sure we have to do this?" she asked, her eyes begging him to say they didn't have to consummate their marriage.

"I'm sorry; we can't take the chance that Olivia will find out. If we're going to do this right, we have to go through with it."

"Maybe I should have two glasses of wine."

"We'll order a bottle when we get back to the hotel."

She simply nodded.

***

It was still early when the meal was over, so Colin suggested they take a walk through downtown to see some of the sights. Jayna relieved by the reprieve of starting their wedding night, said that would be nice. When it started getting dark, Colin told her it was time to return to their hotel.

Once there, he stopped in at the bar and ordered a bottle of his favorite wine to take to their room. After the bartender opened it, he stuck the cork back into the bottle, and handed it to Colin. Once he paid for it, they started for their room.

Jayna dreaded their trip back to their room, as all she could think about was what was going to happen once she had that glass of wine. By the time they'd arrived at their room, she thought she was going to pass out.

Colin unlocked the door, and as he pushed the door open. He thought about picking her up to carry her over the threshold, but just as quickly, he changed his mind. The yearning to make love to her was so intense; he decided it wouldn't be a good idea to touch her just yet. So instead, he took a deep breath to bring his raging hormones under control.

He turned on the light, let her enter first, and then he followed behind her. As Jayna stood there looking around the room, Colin took hold of her hand, causing her to jerk.

"I know this isn't going to be easy on you, but I'll be as gentle as I know how."

"I know. I'm not afraid of you; I just upset about what we have to do."

"Let's have that glass of wine."

"Okay."

Colin went to the counter where the glasses were and turned two over. He removed the cork from the bottle, and then poured each of them a glass of wine. He picked the glasses up, walked over to where she stood and handed her one. He clink his glass against hers. "To my beautiful bride and to us having a wonderful marriage."

Tears filled her eyes. "Thank you, that was beautiful."

When each of their glasses was empty, Colin refilled them. When she finished her second glass, he took it from her and set it on the counter. When he returned to her, his eyes never leaving hers, he removed her jacket. He pulled the tail out of her skirt and started unbuttoning her blouse. He kept waiting for her to stop him, but she didn't nor did she help him.

When he finished with the last button, he pushed the blouse off her shoulders, then threw it towards her suit jacket without seeing if it reached the chair or not. He put his hands behind her and unbuttoned her skirt, and then slowly unzipped it. When the skirt dropped to the floor, he could only stand there and stare at her in her bra and lacey underwear.

Jayna reached out and put her hands on the top button of his shirt. She took a deep breath, telling herself she could do this, and then unbuttoned the first button. When his shirt's buttons were undone, she pushed it off his shoulders. When her eyes took in the muscles showing through his white T-shirt, she swallowed hard.

Watching her eyes, Colin realized she'd been shocked at seeing him without a shirt, as he knew Monroe hadn't had a body like his. These muscles were the result of hours of working out, something you couldn't get while sitting behind a desk as he did all day. Knowing she was in a daze, he grabbed his T-shirt and pulled it over his head.

When Jayna saw his bare chest, she gasped at the sight of his toned chest. When he started undoing his pants, she wanted to turn away, but she didn't. When he dropped his pants, she was surprised to see he was wearing bikini underwear, instead of the white jockey shorts like the ones Monroe wore.

Her eyes flew to his groin, and when she saw the outline of his erection through the cotton material, she quickly turned her back to him. She couldn't do this; she simply couldn't have sex with a man she hadn't seen since she was a kid, especially one who had been friends with Monroe. "Colin, I can't go through with this."

When Colin touched her arms, she jumped. "I'll turn off the lights; you go ahead and get into bed."

"Please Colin, I beg of you. Don't make me have sex with you."

Colin pulled her back against his chest, his erection resting between the cheeks of her bottom. "I'm sorry, truly I am, but we haven't any choice. Now take off the rest of your clothes and get into the bed," he gently told her. Part of him felt bad for what was about to transpire, but the other part couldn't wait to make her his woman.

He went to the light switch and turned it off, and once his eyes became accustomed to the darkness he headed towards the bed. Once there, he removed the last piece of clothing before getting in bed. After he got in, he moved over until his body was up against Jayna's naked body.

"Jayna, I swear if there was another way, I would do it."

"I know."

"I'm going to touch you now."

"Okay." She may have said okay, but when she felt his hand touch her breast, she started crying.

"Please don't cry."

"What Monroe must be thinking of me being in bed with you," she sobbed.

"He knows this is for the sake of your child. I'm going to kiss you now," he said, as he couldn't wait another second to feel her lips against his.

Colin tried to go slowly, but the woman beneath him excited to the point of boiling, and the whole experience was over in less than three minutes flat. He wished he could ask to make love to her second time, but knew he wouldn't be able to do that again for a very long time.

***

When the sexual act was over, she curled into a ball, tears poured down her cheeks, as the experience had been worse than she had thought it would be. She had just let a man, one she barely knew; touch her in the most intimate way that only Monroe had touched before. She felt like a whore, selling her body in the hope of saving her child from its grandmother's plans for him. What made the situation even worse was that she had enjoyed Colin's lovemaking.

Colin moved away from her, as he was unsure how to comfort her. He felt simply awful at knowing he was the cause of her tears, but he had done what he'd thought was best for their situation. "Can I get you anything?"

"No, you've done enough" she replied coldly. She wasn't so much mad at him, as she was at herself. His lovemaking had been so wonderful; she'd been tempted to ask him to do it again. If hadn't been for the fact Monroe hadn't been gone long, Jayna would have liked to have Colin make love to her every night for the next twenty years. That wasn't going to happen again for quite some time, as this was just a business deal, not a love match.

When she left from the bed, he remained quiet, waiting to see if she would return on her own accord. As he listened to her movement, he realized she was getting her nightgown out of her suitcase, and was greatly relieved she wasn't putting her clothes back on. The bed moved as she climbed back in and as he waited for her speak to him, his eyes closed and soon fell asleep.

Jayna laid as far to the edge of the bed as possible, facing away from Colin. As sleep claimed her, her body betrayed her, as it slowly moved closer to his, until they were touching skin to skin.

CHAPTER NINE

When Jayna opened her eyes the next morning, she was shocked to see herself nestled in Colin's arms. Knowing she had to get out of bed before Colin woke and found her in this position, she gently took hold of his arm that rested across her body, and slowly moved it backwards to his side. She lifted her head off his arm, and then started repositioning her torso to the edge of the bed. When her legs reached the side of the bed, thinking she'd accomplished her goal, she sighed.

But when she tried to stand, she found she couldn't because her gown was stuck on something. She quickly turned to see what the problem was, and as her eyes followed her gown, she was surprised to see the end of her gown was being held by Colin's hand.

"Going somewhere?"

She grimaced. "How long have you been awake?"

"Do you really want to know?"

"Yes, I do, otherwise I wouldn't have asked," she replied hatefully.

"I've been awake for the last twenty minutes."

"Oh," she muttered, her face turning crimson.

Colin gave her a wink. "So you see I know how your body was snuggled up tightly against mine."

She grabbed the end of her gown and pulled hard. "A gentleman wouldn't have mentioned that fact."

"Whoever said I was a gentleman, lied to you."

Her eyes flared with anger. "Monroe never lied to me."

Colin suddenly felt bad for teasing her. "I'm sorry Jayna. I shouldn't be tormenting you about any of this."

Tears started forming as she sat there on the bed. "No, *I'm* sorry. You've tried to make this easy on me, but I haven't been very gracious to you."

Colin scooted to the edge of the bed and took hold of her hand. "The hard part is over. Now we'll go back home and tell the Regans that we're married."

"You make it sound so easy."

"What court of law is going to take a child away from its mother and stepfather and give it to the grandmother?"

"One that Olivia has control of, that's who."

"Your father-in-law won't let her do that. As I said before, I've known Mr. Regan all my life. Do you think he's the kind of man that would steal a child from his mother?"

"No, Mr. Regan isn't like his wife. Monroe told me stories about his parents and their marriage, and what I can't understand is why Mr. Regan has stayed with her all these years."

"She blackmailed him," he told her, as he didn't see why she should know the truth.

"What?" she gasped. "How did she do that?"

"His grandfather's loan was at her father's bank, and she threatened to have him foreclose on Albert's loan if Chris didn't marry her."

"That's awful."

"Yes it is. Let's have some breakfast and start for home."

"Okay."

When they left the hotel to eat breakfast, she was relieved to be leaving this place behind and the horrible memories of their breathtaking night together. On the trip home, her mind kept returning to their lovemaking, making her feel even more disloyal to Monroe's memory.

***

It was decided that they would confront Olivia before they drove to her apartment to get some of her belongings. She hadn't moved everything to the apartment yet, so it wouldn't take long to move all her belongings back to the ranch.

When Colin walked up to the front door of the Regans' home, Jayna expected him to knock, so when he put his hand on the doorknob as if to open the door, she gasped. She knew they plan to confront Olivia as soon as they returned home from Arkansas, but she assumed Colin would have at least waited for someone to answer the door.

"Colin, what are you doing? You just can't barge into Olivia Regan's home."

He had to laugh at Jayna's shocked expression. "I want to surprise Olivia and this is the best way to do so," he uttered. He turned the knob, then taking hold of her hand and they entered the house together.

Jayna tried to pull her hand away, but he just tugged her with him and headed towards the dining room. When they stepped into the room, Jayna saw her ex-in-laws were eating their lunch. As she looked at what they were eating, she was stunned at how different the food on their plates was, as Chris had a simple sandwich, and Olivia was eating a more elaborate meal.

According to their plans, Colin was supposed to deliver the message about their marriage, so she waited for him to drop the bomb.

When Olivia saw them standing there, she stood with her fists tightly clinched. "Who are you to barge into my home?" Olivia roared at Colin. She quickly turned to her husband, shocked to see he didn't seem upset to see this stranger with Jayna in their home. "Chris, don't just sit there, call the police."

"You mean to say your daughter-in-law isn't welcomed in your home?" Colin asked her with a smart-alecky grin.

"No and neither are you, so remove yourself from my home," Olivia screeched.

"My name is Colin Sparkman, and since your husband is my father, I'm not leaving unless he asks me too."

Both women let out a loud exclamation of shock at his statement.

Colin turned to his father. "Dad, I'm sorry about blurting it out that like that, but it's important for Olivia to know up front what she's up against."

"Chris is your father?" Jayna squeaked. Tears filled her eyes, at realizing she'd been had by the man she married yesterday. "I don't understand. Monroe never mentioned he had a half-brother," Jayna uttered, confused by what was going on.

Colin turned to face Jayna. "I'm sorry I didn't tell you. I wanted to, but I was too afraid if I told you, you would refuse to marry me, and I really wanted you to be my wife." He turned back to Olivia. "I want you to know that Jayna and I were married yesterday. Now that Jayna's child is mine, I'm going to do anything in my power to prevent you from stealing her child," he stated proudly.

"Way to go Colin." Chris quickly stood and moved to where the two newlyweds were standing.

"Congratulation on the wedding," he said as he hugged Jayna and then his son.

"Chris Regan, is what he says true? Is he your son?" Olivia asked, as this couldn't be possible. How could he have a child by another woman?

"Yes, he's my son, the same as Monroe was," he stated, not caring what was going on in that crazy mind of hers.

"That can't be possible," Olivia screamed at Chris. "I would have known about him as the private investigator I hired would have told me if you were seeing a woman behind my back."

Chris wasn't bit surprised that she'd hired someone to spy on him. "I would demand my money back if I were you, as I spent every Wednesday and all my vacations with Elena for over twenty years," he uttered boldly.

She was shocked by his announcement, and hurt to know another woman had his love all these years. "Did you know about this marriage?" his wife screamed at him as she pointed at the young couple.

He gave her a cold look. "No, I didn't know my son was going to marry Monroe's widow before you did. When I learned you planned to take Jayna's baby from her to punish her for marrying our son, I was sick. I think it's despicable you thought your grandchild could replace Monroe. I told Colin to do whatever he could to save Jayna and her son, as I'm not going to stand by and let you *steal* Jayna's child from her."

"She stole *my* son from me," she screamed at him.

Chris laughed. "Monroe was a young man, not some child she kidnapped from you. A grown child is supposed to leave their parents to start a life of their own. If you think Jayna stole your son from you, then you're more delusional than I thought you were."

"You can't talk to me like that, I'm your wife."

Once again Chris laughed. "Not for long as I have already started divorce proceeding."

"You can't divorce me," she screamed at him.

Chris laughed at her statement. "Of course I can, Olivia. You blackmailed me into marrying you because of my grandfather's loan, which I can happily say has recently been paid off."

"I did what I had to," she stated as if she had the right to force Chris to marry her.

"No, you did what you wanted, and since you'd forced me into marrying you, you thought you'd won. I may have married you, but I never loved you."

"I did win. My son was your heir," she said, smiling an evil smirk.

Colin gave Olivia an ornery grin. "For your information I was *conceived* before Monroe, three months to be exact," Colin said, as he quickly interrupted before his father could say reply to her statement.

"Olivia looked over at her husband. "He's lying."

"No Olivia, Colin's telling the truth. Elena and I were going to get married when you lied to your parents you were pregnant with my child. Of course, by the time they realized you'd lied to them, Monroe was on the way. If it hadn't been for your lies, I would have been married to the woman I loved for the last two decades."

"I loved you and thought we were going to get married. Next thing I know, you're telling me it was over and you went on your merry way."

"That's because it was over. When your father threatened to call in my grandfather's loan on his ranch if I didn't marry you, Elena refused to marry me." He fought back his anger. "So, I married you, something I've regretted every day for the last twenty-five years. Monroe wasn't created out of our love for each other, but conceived while I was under the influence of whatever drug you gave me. And since *our* son is dead, I refuse to live you a minute longer."

"You can't just leave me. What grounds do you have?"

Chris just shook his head. "I don't need grounds."

She was furious by her husband's words, so she struck back at him. "I just wonder what Monroe would have thought if he knew his friend was his father's bastard?"

Chris chuckled at her comment. "My sons met when they were five years old, and for your information, Monroe was thrilled that Colin was his brother."

"Fine, you won. Now will you all get out of my house," Olivia screamed at the three people in front of her, "and take that tramp with you."

"I'm not a tramp," Jayna stated loudly, keeping her head high and her back straight.

"My son's been gone for less than a week, and you're already sleeping with another man. You have slept with him, haven't you?" she asked with an evil tone, as her eyes watched Jayna closely to see if her answer would be a lie.

"I married Colin to protect my child from landing in your greedy hands, you cold-hearted bitch," she replied, feeling a lot better now that she'd called her mother-in-law a bad name. "And for your information, we consummate our marriage in order to protect my child from you."

"You're worse than a tramp," she screamed at Jayna.

Jayna was too shocked by Olivia's newest insult to come up with another one of her own.

When Colin looked over at Jayna, he was saddened by her hurt expression at Olivia's comment. He turned to his father. "We'll talk later." After his father nodded, he took hold of Jayna's hand. "Come on," Colin said, and then pulled her out of the house.

She was crying by the time he closed the front door, so he pulled her into his arms. "I'm sorry she called you names, but she's angry at me."

"Well so am I," she uttered, her eyes snapping with anger.

He gave her a questioning look.

"Don't act as if you don't know why I'm upset," she said, pulling her hand away from his. "You should have told me about your relationship with Monroe as soon I mentioned my problem. You definitely should have told me who your father was when you suggested we get married."

"You're right on all counts, but I was afraid if I told you all that, you wouldn't have married me."

"You're right, I wouldn't have," she shouted at him, tears running down her cheeks.

"I was afraid if I told you Olivia was married to my father; I would have lost your trust."

"Well that didn't go so well, because you *have* lost my trust. Now that I know your father isn't in on Olivia's plan, I'm not worried she'll try to take my baby away from me. And because of that fact, I'm going to file for a divorce."

"I wouldn't bet on that one," he said with a knowing smirk.

His words caused her to panic. "Are you going to stop me?" she asked, stunned by his statement.

"No, but Olivia isn't going to give up just because you're married to her husband's bastard son."

"But that's why we got married. You said that getting married was the best way for me to keep my child. Was that a lie too?" she asked, her petrified eyes staring at him.

"No *that* wasn't a lie, but have you ever seen an angry bee?" he asked, watching her expression closely.

"Well, sure, who hasn't," she replied, unsure why he was talking about bees.

"Olivia is like an angry bee, she's out to sting anyone who has wronged her, and that would be the two of us. Dad can help protect us, but it's going to be a power play on whose friends are more powerful."

"So you're saying we have to stay married."

"Yes, I am."

"Can you tell me why you think so?"

"Olivia doesn't like to lose, so she isn't going to give up until she goes to court. If we're lucky, she'll lose, but even then, she might not give up trying to get custody of her grandchild. So where do you want to go now?"

"Take me to my apartment so I can pick up a few things that I need to take back to the ranch for now, the rest we can move later."

"What are we going to do with the apartment?" he asked, almost afraid she would say she wanted to keep it for later.

"Move whatever we want to keep to the ranch, then sell or donate the rest."

"Don't you want to keep the apartment for after the divorce?"

"No, you and I made a deal. Just because I'm angry at you for not revealing the truth about Chris being your father, doesn't mean I have the right to break it."

Colin was thrilled with her reply. "I'm sorry I didn't tell you before we were married."

She just scrunched her shoulders, as she didn't know how to respond, as she was still upset with him.

The pair was quiet the rest of the way to her apartment, each wondering where this marriage of theirs was going to take them.

***

Meanwhile in the other Regan house, another type of conversation was going on.

"You aren't serious about divorcing me," she said, with panic in her voice.

Chris pulled the envelope he had laying under his newspaper and handed it to her. "It's all in there."

"I'll fight it."

"You can, but it won't do any good."

"I'll bring Elena into it."

"Go ahead. I'm not changing my mind, as your threats can't hurt me any longer. Since our son's dead, there isn't any reason for us ever to speak again." Chris turned and walked out of the room, as Olivia screamed obscenities at him.

***

Figuring Jayna and Colin were the reasons Chris had left her, Olivia was going to make sure they both paid for their interference in her marriage. She wasn't worried that Jayna had married Colin, because it didn't put a crimp in her plans of getting Monroe's child, as she had a sure thing in her pocket.

Her good friend, Judge James would give her custody of her grandchild after he was born, because she knew some of his darkest secrets from when they were younger, secrets he wouldn't want the world to know.

Olivia smiled one of her evil grins, as she would have her revenge on them all when she got custody of Monroe's child, as she would move away and none of them would ever see the child again.

***

When Chris reached his bedroom, he closed and locked the door. He packed several suitcases with his clothes, his shaving kit, and all his personal belongings, which wasn't much. The last thing he did before he left the room was to pick up the picture of his two sons together from that summer they spent together when they were five. Tears formed at seeing how happy the two boys were at knowing they were brothers.

After he finished putting it in the suitcase, he zipped it close and picked it up. He looked around his bedroom once more, glad that he wouldn't ever have to return to this horrible place. When Chris went to the front door, he was relieved not to have to see Olivia. When he was in the car, he took out his cell phone and dialed Elena's number.

"Hello?"

"Elena, I'm packed and about to leave the house."

"I'm so excited that you're moving in with me."

"Me too. I love you, Elena."

"And I love you. Now get your butt over here."

"I'll hurry," he said, never mentioning to her that their son had eloped with Monroe's widow.

***

When Colin pulled away from Monroe's apartment complex, she naturally assumed they were going to the ranch, but when he pulled into the complex next door, Jayna looked over at him.

"What are we doing here?"

"My mother lives here."

"She does? Monroe never told me that," she replied softly, then she had to laugh as there was a great deal he hadn't told her. "Never mind."

Colin smiled at her. "I'd moved into the complex first. When Monroe asked me to look for a place for him to live, wanting to be close to my brother, I rented him an apartment in the other building. Shortly after that, when my mother decided to move here from Ohio, she moved into this one," he told her as he watched for her reaction to his statement.

Jayna just stared at Colin. "Okay, so why are we here?"

"I need to tell her about us."

"Well she's in for a surprise, that's for sure," Jayna said hatefully as she opened her car door to get out.

Colin wanted to say something to her that would make things better between them, but nothing came to mind, so he remained silent.

When they reached the door to his mother's apartment, Colin knocked on it. When Elena opened the door, she'd been expecting Chris, so she was surprised to see her son and Monroe's widow standing there instead. She stuck her head out the door and looked down the hall towards the door to the complex, then looked back at her son.

"What's wrong?" Colin asked his mother.

"Nothing," she replied, with Jayna standing there she couldn't very well say Monroe's father was coming to move in with her.

"Mom, can we come in?"

"Sure, I'm sorry." She stepped back to let the young couple in, hoping they would be gone before Chris arrived; otherwise, she would have to explain to Jayna about her relationship with her father-in-law.

"Jayna, this is my mother, Elena Sparkman. Mom, this is Jayna Sparkman, my bride," he announced proudly.

"Oh, Colin, you didn't," Elena cried, as she knew how her son had fallen in love with Jayna all those years ago.

Colin was completely unprepared for his mother's reply, as his father had been so happy for him. "Mom,

Olivia wanted custody of Monroe and Jayna's baby. Marriage was the only way I knew how to prevent that from happening."

Elena looked over at Jayna. "Is that true?" she asked with disbelief.

"Yes, she said I stole her son from her, so she was going to take my child from me."

"You're fooling yourself if you think marrying Jayna is going to protect Jayna's child. Olivia is a crazy vindictive woman, who will do whatever possible to get her way."

Just then, there was a knock on the door. Elena looked over at the door, then back at her guests.

Colin seeing the panic in his mother's eyes, became concerned that something was wrong. "Do you want me to get it?"

Elena shook her head, as she took hold of Jayna's hand. "Before I open the door, I want you know that will be Monroe's father."

Jayna smiled at her. "I know that Chris is Colin's father too."

Elena's eyes grew wide with astonishment. "You do?"

“We stopped at the Regans’ home first, as we wanted Olivia to be aware that we’re married.”

The knock at the door sounded again, this time louder. Knowing it was his father was on the other side of the door, Colin went to answer it.

“About time,” Chris said automatically as the door opened. When he saw who was standing there, he took a step back. “Colin, what are you doing here?”

“I bought Jayna over to introduce her to Mom.”

Chris stuck his head in through the door to where the two women were standing. “So how did your mother take the news?”

“She disapproved until I told her why we got married. Knowing we were trying to protect the baby made all the difference to her, but she doesn’t think it’s going to matter to Olivia.”

“Knowing Olivia the way I do, I have to agree,” he said as he entered the apartment.

The men joined the woman, and Jayna soon knew all there was to know about Monroe and Colin’s relationship, including the father they had shared all these years.

After the visit with Colin’s parents, they started for the ranch, which was now *their* home. When the newlyweds arrived at the ranch, they informed Albert what they had done and why.

Albert was thrilled at their news, as he knew Colin hadn't married Jayna just to protect his brother's child. He knew it was because he'd fallen in love with Jayna, the same as Monroe had that summer. When they told him that Chris had moved in with Elena, Albert cried, ecstatic that his grandson was finally with the woman he loved.

CHAPTER TEN

The night of Monroe's murder, Christa had been helpless in comforting her sister, as what could she say that could make this situation any easier for Jayna. She'd planned to tell her sister about the baby she and Harrison would be having in six months, but then there was the shooting and her sister was in too much pain to hear her news.

Christa remained quiet about the baby, thinking it would be best to wait and give her sister time to grieve Monroe. But when Jayna up and married Colin, Christa refused to speak to her sister for her lack of respect for Monroe, the man Jayna had loved since she was a teenager.

Jayna was torn up by her twin's attitude towards her. Colin knowing it was up to him to explain to Christa about her sister's rushed wedding to him went to Christa's home without his wife knowledge.

Once he enlightened her to the reason behind Jayna marrying him, Christa forgave her sister, as she understood her wanting to protect her unborn son from Monroe's mother. When she called Jayna, so excited to be talking to her sister once more, she forgot to mention she was expecting a baby too.

The family assumed Jayna would be able to win her case, but when they learned that Judge James was going to preside over the trial, they lost all hope, as they knew he and Olivia had been friends for many years.

Knowing the news of who the judge was on her case had to be upsetting for Jayna; Christa had to check on her sister. Not only that, it was time for her to tell Jayna about the baby she and Harrison was having, so she drove over to her sister's home.

Jayna hearing someone knocking, she put down her paintbrush, and hurried to the door. When she saw her sister, she quickly opened the storm door.

"Come in. What are you doing here? Shouldn't you be at work?"

"I'm on my lunch break." Seeing all the light yellow paint on Jayna's tee shirt, Christa didn't have to ask what Jayna had been doing. "Just came to talk to you, do you have time?"

Jayna's face lit up. "Sure. You look like a woman on a mission."

"Yes, of a matter of fact I am."

"Let me fix us a glass of tea."

After pouring two glasses of the tea, she sat down at the table with her sister."

"So what's up?"

Christa took hold of Jayna's hand. "We're pregnant."

Jayna jumped up and hugged her sister. "That's wonderful. When is the baby due?"

"In six months, same as yours."

Jayna laughed. "I can't believe it. Maybe our babies will be born on the same day."

Christa giggled. "Don't hold your breath, as we both know they come when they want to and not a minute sooner."

"I can still hope."

"How are things going with you and Colin?" Christa asked, hoping Jayna would say that she'd forgiven Colin for not telling her about his relationship with her father-in-law, but the last she'd heard, she wasn't even talking to her husband.

"Colin is working very hard at trying to have Judge James removed from the case, telling the committee that the judge has a conflict of interest since he's good friends with Olivia."

"That sounds hopeful. Do you think it's going to work?"

Jayna simply shook her head. "I doubt it, as Judge James carries a lot of power. He's stating he can be impartial of the outcome of the case, but we don't think he can."

"Jayna, earlier, I was asking about your relationship with your husband, not about your case against your mother-in-law. Are you two even talking?"

Tears filled her eyes as she looked at Christa. "I had loved Monroe since we were teenagers; he was my husband and the father of my baby. I was so happy and in love, then suddenly he was taken from my life. When Colin suggested we get married, Monroe was barely cold in his grave. I thought I could live with myself, but after we had sex, I felt cheap as he caused emotions in me that I feel are wrong because," Jayna started, but when she began crying, she was unable to finish her sentence.

Christa quickly pulled her into her arms. "I know you feel guilty that you're attracted to Colin, but Monroe would want you to be happy."

"I feel like I've been unfaithful to Monroe."

"I can tell you that in watching Colin wherever the two of you are together; I see that he does care for you. Maybe even as long as that summer when we were kids."

Jayna was stunned by her statement. "You don't really think that do you?"

"Yes, I do, as I remember him always watching you even back then."

Jayna laughed. "I was only a kid back then."

"That's when Monroe fell in love with you, so why not Colin?"

"I guess you could be right."

"I also think he loves you, because I don't think most men would have married their sister-in-law just to protect her unborn child like he did. Did you know he came to me and explained why you had married him?"

"He did? He never mentioned that he had talked to you," Jayna replied, puzzled why he hadn't told her. "I just assume you have forgiven me because were sisters."

"You have to respect a man who is willing to take all the blame for what happened."

Jayna nodded. "I'm torn at what to do about my marriage. Maybe I'm using the fact Colin was Monroe's brother to punish the both of us because of the sexual feelings I have for him."

"Jayna, from what I know of Colin, he loved his brother and is grieving too. Maybe he went about things with you the wrong way, but he had the best intention in mind."

"I know."

"Then forgive him and try to make your marriage work, or divorce him and let him move on with his life."

Jayna nodded. "I promise as soon as this ordeal with Olivia is over, I'll do something about my marriage."

"I wouldn't wait that long if I was you, as you may lose a wonderful man in the meantime. I need to get back to work."

The two sisters said their good-byes. As Christa returned to her car, she just hoped that Jayna and Colin could make their marriage work because if her sister happened to lose her baby to her mother-in-law, she was going to need Colin at her side even more.

***

They finally got some good news regarding Jayna's legal matter. Not only had Judge James been removed from the case, but also because of that fact, Olivia had dropped her request for custody of her grandchild. The family celebrated their victory, and with that, victory came the time for Jayna to decide what to do about her marriage.

Still torn between grieving for Monroe and yearning for her present husband, Jayna wasn't sure how to change the status of her marriage. She and Colin had been living in the same house, but with them sleeping in separate bedrooms, there wasn't much of a chance of making their marriage work.

Other than conversing about her legal case, the two didn't speak much to each other. Colin spent long hours at work, and when he did come home, Jayna was already in her bedroom with the door shut.

Albert was torn as seeing the two at odds. Unable to help them work at saving their marriage, he began making plans to move out in the hopes the two could reconcile if he wasn't in the home with them.

***

With Jayna's case against her mother-in-law was finally over, Colin knew so was his marriage. Wanting this to be easier on Jayna, he wrote up their divorce papers, and being that she was having his nephew, he made provisions to provide child support for him until he finished college.

With the paper in hand, Colin went home at a decent hour. When he walked into the door, he was relieved to see Jayna was sitting in the living room instead of her bedroom.

Hearing the door opening, Jayna looked up. Seeing Colin standing there with a distressing expression, she figured he had bad news to tell her, stood, and rushed to him.

"What's wrong?" she asked as she grabbed hold of each of his arms.

Colin's words wouldn't come, as all he wanted to do was pull her into his arms and kiss her as if his life depended on it. He didn't want to end his marriage, but he had to let her go so they could start over and try again.

"Colin, please tell me."

"Where's Albert?" he asked, stepping away from her.

She let her hands drop to her side. "He went out to dinner with your parents."

"Let's go sit down."

She went to the dining room and he followed behind her. When he reached the table, he set his briefcase down on it, opened it, and quickly pulled out the paperwork that would end their marriage. He looked up at her, his eyes full of tears at knowing he was about to lose the only woman he'd ever loved. "Now that your case is over, you'll want this," he said, then handed her the divorce papers.

She took the paperwork from him, and when her eyes saw what it was, she let go of it and it floated to the floor. "Is this what you want?" she asked him softly, as tears filled her eyes. Christa had been right, she was losing the man she'd come to love.

"You know it isn't. I want to stay married to you and raise a houseful of children together."

She laughed despite her sadness of him bring home divorce papers. "I don't think I want a houseful, but I'm willing to give you at least one more child," she said bravely, as last night she'd concluded that she wasn't going to fight her attraction to him any longer.

"You mean it?" he asked, almost too afraid to ask.

"Colin, I'm sorry I've been such a bitch to you. You've given up so much in order to protect my child," she said as she put her hand on her belly, "while I haven't given you anything but heartache."

"You had a right to be angry at me for not being truthful of my relationship with Chris and Monroe. I handled it all wrong and for that I'm sorry."

"I forgive you, but don't you ever hold back the truth from me again."

He took hold of her arms and pulled her into his arms. "In that case, I want you to know that I love you and want you to be my wife."

She giggled. "Colin, we're already married."

"No, not really. I want us to have a real wedding, one where neither of us feels as if we're doing it for all the wrong reasons."

She gave him a smile. "You mean one that I don't feel pressured into."

He gave her a lopsided grin. "I really didn't give you much of a choice in the matter."

"No, but you were trying to protect my son from Olivia, and I do appreciate all you did for me."

"Since you want honesty, then I must tell you I didn't marry you just for that reason."

"Colin, I know that now, but at the time, I was still grieving the loss of Monroe and didn't see the other reason why you were willing to marry me."

"I guess if I had been honest with you then, it would have saved us some heartache."

"I had loved Monroe since I was a thirteen, so it's going to take some time for me to heal from his death, but with your help, I'm sure we can put him to rest and make our marriage work."

"I would like that."

"I'm not ready to sleep with you again just yet, but if we work at our relationship, we'll eventually get there."

"I'm willing to try if you are."

She put her hand out to him, but instead of taking hold of her hand, he pulled her into his arms and brought his lips to hers. Instead of fighting against his embrace, she stayed in his arms and simply enjoyed the moment.

***

It was the month before Jayna and Christa's babies were due and everything was going great for the two sisters. Christa didn't think her life could get any better, but then she was informed that her husband had been killed in a car accident.

When Harrison's body was taken to the morgue, the attendant called and told Christa that he thought it would be best if someone other than herself identified the body. She didn't even think twice about it, but simply called Colin and asked for his help.

Colin and Jayna drove to Christa's house so that they could drive her to the hospital. Harrison's death brought back all the horrors Jayna had gone through when Monroe had died, so she knew what her sister was experiencing. When they entered the house, Jayna gave her sister a tight hug, and the two had a good cry together.

Jayna told her sister that she was welcomed to move out to the ranch, as she had been there for her, so now it was her turn to comfort Christa. She responded that she wasn't sure what she wanted to do just yet.

While the two women stayed in the lobby, Colin went to identify the body of his brother-in-law. When he entered the room and saw Harrison's face, he was glad he was viewing the body instead of Christa. If it hadn't been for the fact that the man was wearing the shirt he and Jayna had given him for his birthday, and his driver's license found in the wallet, Colin wouldn't have guessed the man on the table was Harrison.

He told the attendant that because of the damage to his face, he couldn't swear the man was Harrison Ashby, but it was likely that it was. Considering the circumstances, who else could he be?

When Colin returned to the lobby, he sat down next to Christa and took hold of her hand. He then had the horrible job of telling her about her husband. He explained that the body was too damage to make a positive identification, but because he'd been found outside of *his* car, with his driver's license on him, wearing a shirt he recognize, it must be Harrison.

"He was so excited about the baby, now he'll never get to see our child."

"Colin and I will help you as much as we can."

Christa laughed. "You're going to be busy with a baby of your own. You won't have time to be helping me with mine."

"If you move back to the ranch, we can make sure you and your little one are taken care of."

"Thank you for the offer, but I don't want to intrude."

"Albert would love having you back on the ranch. If you don't want to live with us, I'm sure Grayson would love you and the baby to live with him."

"Let me think on it for a few days. First, I need to tell Harrison's father about his death, that we were married and I'm having his grandson." She sobbed. "I also have to make arrangement for Harrison's funeral, but I'm not sure where to start."

"Colin and I will help you with that."

And they did, as well as all the other necessary things that needed to be done.

In the end, Christa decided to stay in her own home. That first night alone, she stepped into the baby's room and looked around. Harrison had already painted the baby's room a light green, and the furniture was all set up, just waiting for her to bring their son home to it. She went to the rocking chair in the corner and sat down, then rocked as she cried for the loss of her husband.

***

The next month seemed to drag for the two mothers-to-be. When Jayna's labor started the day before her due date, she was thrill that her son was going to be born before her sister's son was. Then she felt bad, as Christa was all alone, while she had Colin for support. The two sisters had promise to call the other when the time came, so Jayna called Christa.

"Hello?"

"Christa, I just want you to know that Colin and I are on our way to the hospital."

At her sister's words, Christa's heart dropped, as she was envious that her sister had been first. "I'll be there as soon as I can."

"If you don't feel up to it, I'll understand."

"No, I want to be there. Have you called Chris and Elena yet?"

"Colin's doing that while I call you."

"Colin's parents sure did have a beautiful wedding. To believe Elena waited all these years for Chris. That's what you call *true love*," she said with a tear-filled voice.

"Christa, Harrison loved you just as much."

"Yes, he did. I hate having this baby without him."

"I know and I wish he was at your side too. Is Mr. Ashby still denying that you and Harrison were married?"

"Yes. Even though he'd seen the marriage license, he says I'm trying to pull a scam on him. How am I doing that? It isn't as if I'm asking for any money from him, I just want him to acknowledge that I'm having his grandson."

"At least, Mr. Ashby didn't try to prevent you from getting Harrison's life insurance, so maybe he's coming to terms with the reality that his son and you were married. Maybe after the baby's born and he sees him, he'll accept what you've been telling him."

"I really don't care what he thinks, as I know who the father of my baby is."

"Christa, we'll talk more later, as we need to be leaving for the hospital."

***

When Christa arrived at the hospital, the waiting room was already filled with the rest of their family, which of course included Albert. Happy to see the old man, she went to where he was sitting; he stood and gave her a hug.

When Chris and Elena saw Christa, they joined her and each gave her a hug. When Chris asked how she was feeling, she said she felt pregnant, causing everyone in the room to laugh. Two hours later, Colin came out and announced that they had a healthy baby. The group stayed only long enough to grab a peak of the newest member of the family, and then left the new parents alone with their baby.

CHAPTER ELEVEN

When Christa had returned to her apartment from the hospital, she went to the kitchen to fix herself some tea, but before she could heat the water, she felt something wet run down her legs. When she glanced down at her feet and saw the puddle forming around her feet, she realized her water had broken. A smiled filled her face, as her dream of having her child on the same day as her sister was about to come true.

She reached for the phone to call Dr. Werden to tell him that she was on her way to the hospital. She hadn't cared for the man, as he made her feel uneasy, but since her father-in-law had requested Christa use him, and wanting to keep things pleasant between her and Harrison's father, she didn't change doctors. She should have gone with her gut instinct, as it would have saved her a great deal of pain and heartache in the long run if she had.

When she'd called Dr. Werden and told him the baby was coming, she assumed he would tell her to go on to the hospital, but instead, he said he and his wife were on their way to her house. When she questioned him about it, he told her a home birth would be a more relaxing atmosphere to give birth. One of the last things he told her was that since she and the baby were *healthy*, there wouldn't be any problems with a home delivery.

She'd rather have gone to the hospital, but following her doctor's request, she gave him her address. She was relieved when the doctor and his wife arrived, and the threesome went into her bedroom. While she got into bed, the doctor and his wife started preparing the room for the delivery.

Her labor was quick and with her using the breathing method, she'd learn in her childbirth classes, there was hardly any pain. One minute the doctor was telling her he could see the baby's head, and the next minute, the nurse was giving her a shot.

When she'd asked what the injection was for, she was told it wasn't anything for her to be concerned about and just relax. A short time later, her surroundings started to get fuzzy and she began to feel sleepy. As it pulled her towards slumber, she tried to fight it by keeping her eyes open, but the drug was stronger. Just as she heard her baby cry, she lost the struggle and her eyes closed.

The last things she heard before sleep fully claimed her was the doctor telling someone named Mack, they had a son, and then everything went blank.

When she woke up, Lloyd Ashby was with her, but she didn't see any sign of a baby in the room. "Where's Jeffery?"

Her father-in-law took hold of her hand. "I'm so sorry, but he didn't make it."

"But I heard him crying," she sobbed.

"Yes, I'm sure you did. He started having trouble breathing, the doctor tried to save him, but he wasn't successful."

"I want to see my baby."

"I'm sure you would, but I'm afraid you won't like what you see," he told her, as he forced himself to pat her hand.

She gave him a confused look. "What are you talking about?"

"Jeffery was terribly deformed, so much so, I hate for you to see him. When we have his funeral, the casket will have to be closed."

"Deformed?" If her child had some sort of deformity, it would have showed up on her last sonogram, that and she would have given birth in a hospital instead at her home.

As she looked at her father-in-law's nervous behavior, she became suspicious that something wasn't quite right here. She closed her eyes as she tried to remember her son's birth. Suddenly she remembered the doctor telling someone else that they had a son.

It was then she realized that her father-in-law was lying to her about her son being born deformed and dying. Since Lloyd never believed she was carrying Harrison's baby in the first place, he must have come up with a scheme with the doctor to give her child away so she couldn't claim Jeffery as his grandchild.

As she laid there with her eyes closed, she knew she had to be careful what she did next as Lloyd Ashby was a wealthy man, one who was used to getting his way. She also knew she couldn't confront him just yet, as she didn't have any proof of this switch. And if she did say something now, he could cover her face with a pillow to end her life and no one would ever be the wiser of what he'd done.

She cleared her mind of all her hostilities before she opened her eyes to look at him. "Have you made the funeral arrangements yet?" she asked, watching his face closely for any signs she was on the right track.

Her heart jumped with relief when she noticed a slight relaxing of his face at her words. It was so insignificant, that if she hadn't been watching for it, she would have missed it. To her, this meant her son was alive somewhere out there and she wouldn't stop looking for him until she breathed her last breath.

"Yes, I hope you don't mind."

She gave him an artificial smile. "Thank you, I appreciate you doing that for me."

"Do you have any idea what your plans are now?"

She'd just been told she'd lost her child, her only link to her husband, what did he expect her to say. The thought of living anywhere near this man made her physically sick to her stomach, so staying here was out of the question. She hated leaving her family, but for now, she had to get away for a while. "I'm going to find a job in a different part of the country so I can get away from things that remind me of Harrison."

He nodded. "I think that would be best."

She just bet he thought that. With her gone, he didn't have to worry about being caught by the fact that he'd given her child away to strangers. It might take her awhile, but someday she was going to prove Lloyd Ashby had something to do with her child being taken from her and send him to jail.

***

On the day of the funeral, Christa had crept into the room that Jeffery's funeral was going to be held, as she had to know for sure if her assumption was correct. Seeing the room was empty, she hurried over to the casket and lifted the lid. The infant lying there indeed was disfigured, but as she looked at him, she knew this Hispanic child with the reddish pear-shaped birthmark just above his left eyebrow, couldn't be hers. Her eyes began filling with tears with relief.

Hearing someone walking towards the room, she knew she couldn't leave without being seen, so she quickly closed the lid and rushed over the first row of seats. Once there, she quickly sat down, dropped her head, and let the tears fall.

Anyone seeing the tears would assume they were tears of sorrow, but they were tears of joy, as she now knew for sure that Jeffery was alive. She wasn't sure how she was going to go about it, but some day, she was going to find her son, even if it meant she would have to threaten Lloyd's life to do so.

When Lloyd came into the room, he was startled to see Christa sitting there. His eyes quickly moved to the coffin, and was relieved to see the lid was down. Of course, *if* she had looked inside, she wouldn't be sitting there crying, but screaming at him that the body in the coffin wasn't her son. He walked to where she was sitting and sat down next to her. "What are you doing here all alone?"

She turned and looked at him. "I needed to say good-bye without my family staring at me, watching and waiting for me to breakdown."

Lloyd satisfied by her answer, nodded. "I can understand that. When is your family due to arrive?"

Christa looked at her watch. "They should be walking in the door any minute now. Jayna had to drop her son off at her in-laws before coming."

Before Lloyd could reply, Jayna and Colin entered the room. Christa wanting to get as far away from him as possible, stood, and started towards sister. Just as she reached them, Grayson and Albert came into the room.

After everyone hugged her, the group headed to the front of the room with Jayna leading the way. Jayna knowing how her sister felt about Lloyd, she sat down in a chair on the opposite side of the aisle from him, and her family followed her lead.

The service was a small one and there wasn't a dry eye in the room. Christa hadn't told her family her theory that her son was alive, as she knew her chances of ever finding him was very slim. In fact, she thought the chances were practically impossible, that is unless Lloyd told her where he was.

As soon as the bogus Jeffery Ashby funeral was over, Christa went home and refreshed her resume. Once she was satisfied with it, she started a search for a job somewhere far from Kansas City.

Jayna was upset to learn what she was doing, but she understood Christa wanting to get away from everything that reminded her of her tragic losses, but that didn't stop her from trying to talk her sister out of leaving.

CHAPTER TWELVE

When Olivia's informant told her that Jayna had given birth to Preston, she knew the time to retrieve her grandson had arrive. But before she could act on it, she had to know where all the major players were. First, she called Colin's office and asked to speak to him. When she was told he was in a meeting, she quickly hung up the phone before his assistant could ask if she wanted to leave a message, as that wasn't the reason for her calling.

At this time of day, Chris and that woman he married would be at work and Albert would be gone from the ranch, as it was his day to play bingo at the church, which meant Jayna was home alone with the baby. The time had come for her to put her plan into action.

She packed her car with several suitcases, as once she picked up the baby; she was flying to England on a private jet. Once there, Olivia was changing the baby's name to Fraser, after his grandfather and her name to Betsy Smith, and wouldn't ever return to the United States.

Olivia drove out to the ranch and parked down the road from Jayna's home. She took the gun out of the glove box and tucked in her pocket, and then she got out of the car. Wanting to keep out of sight as much as she could, she moved toward the grove of trees to her right. Once she was hidden among the trees, she started for the house.

When she reached the front of the house, Olivia looked around at the surrounding area. She didn't see any cars outside of the garage, so that meant Jayna didn't have any guests that could interfere with her plans.

There were several cars parked across the road at her brother's house, but they didn't concern her, as he too would be at work. Knowing the coast was clear;

she took the gun out of her pocket and then knocked on the door.

When Jayna answered the door, she was stunned to see Olivia standing there with a gun pointed at her chest. "Olivia, what are you doing here?" she asked, her hand clenching the doorframe for support.

"Aren't you going to ask me if I want to see my grandson?" Olivia asked as she cocked the gun.

Jayna moved back to let her in. "Preston is sleeping at the moment. Why don't you come back later?"

Olivia just laughed as she shut the door behind her. "That won't be necessary as I'm here to take your child from you the same as you did to me."

Panic seized hold of Jayna, as she had a feeling this situation was going to end with someone getting shot, and that person probably was going to be her. "I didn't take your child away from you."

"If you hadn't sneezed that day of the engagement party, then you would have been the one to die instead of my son. That or if the man I hired had been a better shot, then my son would still be with me."

"Oh, my God! Olivia, you're responsible for us losing our son," Chris stated behind her.

Shocked to hear Chris' voice, Olivia spun around. "What are you doing here?" So much for her plan of kidnapping the baby without anyone being aware of it until after she'd left the country with the baby.

"Does it matter why I'm here?" he asked.

"No, it just changes things a bit. I didn't see your car out front."

"That's because it's across the road at Grayson's place. I drove out here with Christa; she's visiting her brother, while I ran over here to check on Jayna." He didn't know why he told her all that, other than he was trying to stall her from leaving.

***

Olivia's original plan had been to shoot Jayna before she left with the baby, but she couldn't shoot Chris because even though he'd divorced her, she still loved him. Since she couldn't kill him, she would have to find a way to keep him from interfering in her plans. She quickly looked around the room to see what she could use to tie these two up, spying the curtain ties, the perfect plan came to her. "Go stand by Jayna," she said, pointing the gun at Chris's chest.

Worried about Olivia's mental state, Chris simply did as she asked, not because he was afraid of dying, but because Olivia might kill Jayna if he didn't do as she asked.

"Jayna, go get those draperies ties and tie Chris up. Make sure they're tight because if they aren't, you won't live to see tomorrow."

Jayna hated having to tie up her father-in-law, but since she didn't have any other choice, she quickly did what Olivia demanded of her.

When Chris was tie up tight, Olivia came up to Jayna, and brought the butt of the gun down hard on the side of her head and she immediately crashed to the floor.

Olivia giggled, her plan may have gotten a bit off track, but she'd accomplished what she came here to do. Now all she had to do was get the baby and get the Hell out of Dodge.

***

Unbeknown to Olivia, Elena was also in the house and as soon as she realized why Olivia was there, she had called the police and informed them about the kidnapping. She hated the fact she couldn't do anything to stop Olivia from taking the baby, but she couldn't take the chance that she would shoot Jayna or Chris.

When Olivia stepped out of the house, high on her excitement of fulfilling her goal, she didn't notice how quiet the area around the house was, as not even a bird was chirping. With her mind on her getting to her car and leaving as fast as she could, she didn't see several high power rifles aimed at her head.

When she reached her car, she opened the back door and put the baby in the car seat she had put in there earlier. When she was satisfied that baby secured, she shut the door, and turned to open her door.

"Olivia Regan, hold it right there," a man's cold stern voice called to her.

Shocked to hear someone calling out her name, she looked up. When she saw the dozen or so police officers' rifles aimed at her, her first reaction was to grab for the gun in her pocket. She had just pulled it out when a gunshot was heard, and a split second later, Olivia lay dead on the ground.

Once she was down, three officers swiftly ran towards the car, two checked to make sure Olivia wasn't going to be causing any more trouble, while the other ensured the baby was unharmed. The officer being a father himself felt very protective of the infant as he took the sleeping child out of his car seat. Once the infant was in his arms, he started towards the house, and just as he reached the front door, it opened, and a slightly stunned Jayna, was reaching for her baby.

***

Olivia's parents were ashamed to learn of all Olivia's evil actions regarding Chris and Jayna, not only on that eventful day when she tried to kidnap Monroe's son, but also that she'd been the cause of their grandson's death. Deciding it would be best to have a quiet funeral for Olivia, they were the only ones in attendance.

After the service, Olivia was put to rest in the burial spot she had originally bought for Monroe, which Chris thought was ironic. And when her tombstone arrived and placed at her gravesite, it would simply have her name, with her birth and death date. It wouldn't have *Beloved Daughter*, *Loving Wife*, or *Wonderful Mother* on it, as Olivia hadn't been any of those things.

***

When Christa was offered a job in St. Louis at Baker's Consultants, she packed up her life, said goodbye to everyone, and then drove east. The consulting company where she was going to be working for was a small one, having only twenty employees. Her function as office manager was to see the running of the office, doing a little bit of everything, from ordering office supplies, talking to irate customers, to manning the phone when the receptionist wasn't available. She came to love her job and her co-workers soon became her family, joining them for special holidays and birthdays.

One sunny summer day, six months after Harrison's death, she was invited to one of the consultant's home. She thought by now she would have started to heal, but she was still having nightmares of the how her little one had been stolen from her just moments after he entered the world. Not wanting to spend time with coworkers and their children, she'd declined the invitation.

Her boss, Henry Sloan told her since he was throwing the surprise party for the Stockwell and

Angela McWilliams' fourth wedding anniversary, he wouldn't take no for an answer. He told her the party was going to be swimming party and to be sure to bring her swimming suit.

Christa thought it was hilarious to be having that kind of a party, as it was winter, with an inch of snow on the ground. When she mentioned she wasn't interested in swimming in icy water, he told her that Stockwell had an indoor pool so he could swim all year around. She thought it must be nice to have so much money that you could have an indoor pool in your home.

***

When she entered the all-glass room, she saw some of the other guests were already in the water. She hadn't brought a swimming suit; as she planned to just sit and watch the others enjoy themselves, stay for an hour, and then quietly sneak out.

She grabbed herself a soda and then went to sit at the farthest table from the pool. As she sat there drinking her beverage, she started watching Stockwell playing with his young son in the water.

Wishing it were her family out there playing together, instead of some other woman's family, she fought the tears. Thinking of the son she'd lost, she was mad at herself, as she still hadn't found a way to prove her father-in-law had stolen him from her the night he was born.

As she continued to watch father and son, she started thinking about how much Brady McWilliams looked like pictures she had of Harrison at that same age. With that thought in her mind, she realized that Angela's son could have been traded with hers, as the woman was definite Hispanic.

Her heart started pounding, wondering if just maybe she'd found proof her son wasn't dead after all. But then she had to shake her head, as she wasn't thinking clearly, she had been in Kansas City when her child had been stolen, not hundreds of miles away in St. Louis. What were the odds of her being in the home of the couple who had her son? Not very high, she would have to say.

Christa jumped when someone sat down next to her, as she'd been so deep in her ramblings thoughts that she hadn't notice anyone walking her way. When she turned and saw Angela, she forced herself not to give away her thoughts. "Angela, you surprised me."

"I notice you staring at my husband," she hissed angrily at her.

Christa was stunned by the woman's cold words, as she'd been starting at the child, not Stockwell. "I'm sorry, but I was wishing it was *my* husband and child out there playing together."

Angela gave her a stunned look. "You want my husband and child?" She was worried that if Stockwell knew the beautiful Christa Ashby was interested in him, he might decide to leave her for the other woman.

Christa put her hand on Angela's arm and gave her a weak smile. "Your husband is a very good-looking man, but I'm not interested in him. You see, I lost my husband in a car accident, and when our child was born a month later, I lost him too," she said just as a single tear dropped down her cheek. She looked back out at the father and son playing. "I was just wishing *my* family was still in my life, not that *your* family was mine."

Angela's heart broke, as she could understand the other woman's pain. "I didn't know. I'm sorry for your loss."

"Thank you." Christa smiled at her, giving Angela's hand a quick squeeze. "It's something I don't usually talk about as it makes people uncomfortable."

"My son is very precious to us."

"I'm sure he is. Did you have a hard labor?" she asked innocently, as the probability of her son being with this family was very improbable.

Angela took another sip of her drink, looked around her, then leaned over to whisper in Christa's ear. "All I had to do was drive to Kansas City."

"You didn't give birth to him?" Christa had to be careful what she asked, as she didn't want Angela to know just how interested she was in her son's parentage.

"No, not to him I didn't." Her eyes looked over at her husband, then back towards Christa.

"Can you tell me what happened?" she asked slowly.

"My doctor had informed me after my second sonogram that my baby was deformed," she started, keeping her eyes on her husband and child to make sure they didn't come over to where they were sitting without her being aware of it.

Those words made Christa give Angela her full attention.

"Stockwell wanted a son so badly that I didn't have the heart to tell him it was likely our son wouldn't even survive his birth. When Dr. Werden called me a month later, he told me he had a client who was giving her child up for adoption and wanted to know if I wanted the baby."

When Christa heard the doctor's name, she grasped hold of her hands to keep them from shaking. Instead of jumping up and running for the nearest police station, she forced herself to remain sitting, as she had to hear the whole story. But once she knew for sure it was her child in the swimming pool, she was going straight to the police.

"When the other woman went into labor, the doctor called me and I flew to Kansas City. The doctor preformed a caesarean on me and the two infants were exchanged and I flew back home with the other woman's baby."

"What happened to your baby?" she asked softly, fighting the tears that were threatening to appear.

"The doctor said he would take care of the burial, as the infant hadn't survived. Please don't tell Stockwell, as he doesn't know the child isn't his."

Christa was relieved to know that Stockwell hadn't been involved with the baby switch. "No, I won't say anything to Stockwell," she said, and she meant it. But that didn't mean she wouldn't be telling the police about the child if she found out for sure he was hers. "How did you keep this secret from your husband?"

"Stockwell was out of town at the time of the delivery and I didn't call him to tell him the baby had arrived until after I returned to St. Louis."

"Did the baby you lost look like either of you?" She knew she shouldn't ask this question, but she had to be certain the baby she saw when she'd peeked into the coffin was the child Angela had left behind.

Her expression turned sad as tears appeared. "Yes, you could see my heritage in him, that and he had the same birth mark just above his eye brow as I have," she said, pulling her bangs back to show Christa.

Christa looked closely at Angela's birthmark, and seeing the pear-shaped mark, she was positive of whose baby her father-in-law had used in place of hers. "Stockwell didn't notice that the child didn't take after you?"

"He was so thrill to have a son that I don't think he even noticed, but if he did, he must have assumed the child took after his side of the family."

When Christa heard someone yell, *Hey Mack*, from the pool, she quickly turned her head towards the voice, and was quite stunned to see the man was talking to Stockwell. She turned back to Angela. "Why did that man call your husband, Mack?"

"Because of our last name."

"Are you ever called *Mack*?"

She laughed. "That's was what Dr. Werden called me, as it was my code name," came the reply.

"Interesting," Christa muttered, as it was all she could think to say. "If you excuse me, I need to go fix my face."

"You go ahead," Angela said, unaware her life was about to change for the worse.

***

Christa went into the house, and after making sure, no one was watching her; she crept upstairs to the bedrooms. As she quietly walked down the hall, she peeked into different rooms until she found the baby's room. She looked behind her, and seeing she was alone, she hurried into the child's room.

Once there she glanced around the room for something with the child's DNA, for once she did, she was taking it to the police to be tested. Hearing someone in the hallway, she knew had to find what she needed and get out of this room. Because if she was found in the baby's room, she didn't know how to explain why she was in here. She glanced around the room, but didn't see anything small enough for her to sneak out of the house.

She'd just about to give up and leave the room, when she happened to see a forgotten pacifier on the floor behind the crib. She hurried over to the crib, pulled it away from the wall, leaned down, and grabbed the pacifier in her hand. When she straightened, she quickly stuck it into her pocket, and then let out a sigh of relief, as the hard part was over.

After moving the crib back in place, she started for the door. As she left the room, she was grinning, for if some miracle Stockwell's child was hers, this pacifier would prove it. Once the authorities knew he was hers, she would have her son back. But first, she had to get out of the house with her evidence before anyone could stop her, otherwise she wouldn't be able to have it tested.

She hurried down the hall to the stairs, and once she reached the ground floor, she went outside and grabbed her purse. She didn't even take time to thank her hosts, as then she would have to explain why she was leaving so suddenly.

The first stop she made was to the local police station, where she was quickly set up with Detective Darrell Tuggle. When she told him, she believed the McWilliams had her child; the detective just gave her a dazed look. She then explained that she believed her father-in-law had traded their deceased child for hers, and that the McWilliams weren't even aware of the baby switch.

He didn't want to believe her story, but he had to do his job, so he started his investigation by having the pacifier test against her DNA. He was quite stunned when the results of the test showed Christa Ashby was the child's mother.

"Mrs. Ashby, since the test shows the child *is* yours, I'm thinking you had an affair with Stockwell McWilliams, and you being single, you let him have custody of the baby. You've since changed your mind and now you want the baby back," Darrell told her.

"No, you have it all wrong. I'm telling you the truth. If you test both of the McWilliams, it'll show they aren't the child's parents."

"If I test Stockwell's DNA and it matches the boy's, will you drop this and leave the McWilliams alone?" Darrell asked.

"I will, but only if you agree that if it doesn't match Stockwell that you'll continue with your investigation," she said with a determined voice.

"Okay you have a deal."

"Then you better prepare to dig up the body in my child's grave, as I'm sure he's the McWilliams' child."

The detective just nodded, as he assumed she was wrong. Once again, he had to do his job, so he called the McWilliams into the station so Stockwell could be tested.

***

"Detective, you want to explain what this is all about," Stockwell demanded.

Darrell looked at the couple for a moment, as he wasn't sure how to proceed.

"Well?" Stockwell asked.

"I need to test your son's DNA to you and your wife."

"Excuse me," Stockwell asked, as he was confused why the officer wanted it.

"We need to verify the young fellow in your arms does belong to you and your wife, as there's a chance your son was swapped with another moments after he was born."

When Darrell saw Angela's face go white, he figured she was aware of the exchange. He quickly looked at Stockwell to check out his expression and saw only confusion.

"I don't understand why we have to prove his our son?"

"We've tested a woman's DNA against a pacifier that she states belongs to your son. Since DNA doesn't lie, the test shows the child belongs to her. If that's true, then you could still be the father."

"I can assure you that if he isn't my wife's child, then he isn't my child either," Stockwell assured him.

"That's why we want to test the three of you."

"Then what?"

"If he turns out not to be your child, you have to turn the child over to Family Services," Darrell waited for the man in front of him to admit he had just lied about fathering the infant, but he just sat there looking sad.

"When?" Stockwell asked.

"As soon as we get the DNA tests back and find the infant isn't your son."

"That's fine with me," he stated, as he was sure the test would show the boy was theirs. "How long will it take to get the test results?"

"We're putting a rush on it and should know back in an hour."

"We'll just go grab some lunch and then we'll be back," Stockwell said as he stood to leave.

In the back of Angela's mind, she was thinking they would take the child and run to Canada, but that thought was soon crushed.

"I'm sorry, but you can't leave this office with the child in question," Darrell told them. "You can order something to be delivered or leave the child here while you go out."

Stockwell was disappointed by his statement, but understood. "We'll just wait to eat until after the results have come in."

CHAPTER THIRTEEN

Detective Tuggle had been completed surprised when the DNA test results arrived and it showed Stockwell and his wife wasn't the child's parents, as he thought Mrs. Ashby had made up the story. Now he had the unpleasant chore of informing the McWilliams that the child they had in their arms, wasn't theirs. Since they'd been waiting in his office, he went to join them.

"Well?" Stockwell asked.

"What I'm about to tell you is going sound crazy, especially for you Mr. McWilliams."

"Why's that?" he asked nervously, afraid what the detective had to tell him.

Darrell took a deep breath. "According to my source, your wife has a secret regarding the birth of your son."

Stockwell looked over at his wife expecting her to deny the man's statement, but she just sat there, looking down at her hands.

"The problem with this secret is that the other person involved in this situation happened to have kept a secret from her."

"Can you explain all this in terms I can understand?" Stockwell said, infuriated at this run around in the explanation.

Darrell looked at Angela. "Do you want to tell him or should I?"

Tear filled eyes looked up at him. "Since you seem to know more about this than I do, maybe you should."

"The story I was told was that a few month ago your wife found out that your child had a deformity, which was so bad that he was going to die because of it."

"There isn't anything wrong with my son," Stockwell stated loudly.

Darrell looked at him, trying to find the right words to continue his story. "That's where you're wrong."

"What are you talking about?"

"I'm sorry to tell you this, but from what I've been told, your son died and the doctor who delivered him, switched your son with another woman's healthy child. The infant you have was stolen from his mother and was given to your wife in exchanged for her dead child."

"The child wasn't stolen," Angela cried out.

Stockwell looked over at his wife as he touched her hand. "That part isn't true, but the rest of his story is?" he asked, his eyes filling with tears at the thought he was going to lose the child he thought was his.

Angela wasn't sure how this detective knew she'd traded their son for another, but it didn't matter now that her husband knew what she'd done. "Oh, Stockwell I'm so sorry. When the doctor told me about our son, I was heartbroken. I was going to tell you, but then my doctor called and told me a woman was giving her son up for adoption and asked if I wanted him."

"And naturally you said *yes*?" he asked softly.

"I did," she said tearful.

"I see." He looked at the detective. "Please continue."

"The child you have is Christa Ashby's child," he told them, and then waited for his words to sink in before continuing.

"We have Christa's child?" This story was getting more far-fetched by the moment. "Are you sure there isn't some sort of mistake?"

"Oh, God," Angela cried. "Now it made since of all Christa's questions regarding Brady and his birth."

"DNA doesn't lie, and his DNA test shows the child belongs to Christa Ashby. I'm sorry but I have to take the child."

"When?" Stockwell asked as he looked down at the boy he thought was theirs.

"Immediately, as in right now." He motioned to someone across the room.

The professional dressed woman came towards them; she didn't smile or acknowledge the McWilliams as she reached for the child. Angela kissed the baby's cheek, and then quietly handed the child to the woman.

The woman took the child, grabbed the diaper bag that Angela had brought with them and simply walked away. She entered another room and the child known as Brady McWilliams was finally reunited with his biological mother.

***

"What happens now?" Stockwell asked while trying not to cry at losing the child they'd loved for the last five months. "Are you going to press kidnapping charges against my wife?" he asked, not really caring either way.

"Christa doesn't think your wife knew the child had been kidnapped, so she isn't pressing any charges. If your wife is willing to give us a statement regarding what she assumed was purely a secret adoption, we won't either. We still need to prove the child in Jeffery Ashby's grave is your son. Once we know for sure, we'll contact you."

Stockwell simply nodded. They didn't touch as they walked to their car, so different from their walk into the station. The car ride was quiet, as there didn't seem to be any words that could fix this situation. If only Christa hadn't been invited to their anniversary party, none of this would have come to light, and the boy would still be theirs. Then he shook his head, as if it hadn't been at this party, he was sure, it would have happened at one of the many others functions the company had throughout the year.

Angela waited until they entered the house before speaking to her husband. "Stockwell, I'm so sorry for everything." She put her hands up to her face and began sobbing. "What are we going to do?"

He wanted to hate her, but right now, he wasn't sure how he felt. His emotions were in turmoil, as he knew Angela's heart had been in the right place when she'd switched their dead child with a live one.

Angela denied knowing anything about the kidnapping, but he felt she was lying. "My heart is aching not only for us, but for what Christa has gone through because of what you did."

"If it hadn't been us, the doctor would have given the baby to someone else."

"I'm sure you're right, but that fact doesn't ease my pain, as Christa was my friend. I think it would be best if I move out for a while to give us time to think about what you did behind my back."

"You're divorcing me?"

"Right now I don't know what to do regarding our marriage." He then turned and went to their bedroom, where he packed a bag of some of his belongings. When he returned to the living room, he started for the front door

"You'll keep in touch, won't you?" Angela asked before he could open the door.

"Yes, I'll call you later in the week." When he left the house, he simply walked out the door without saying anything else to his wife.

Tears fell as Angela watched him leave, as this was the first time in their marriage that he'd ever left without kissing her and telling her that he loved her.

Stockwell checked into a hotel, and then went to his room to unpack. When that chore was done, he laid down on the bed so that he could think about the mess of his life. As he thought of where to go next, he began thinking of Christa. He'd been attracted to her from the first moment she started working at Baker's Consultants. Maybe if he was single, she might be interested in dating him, if so, then Brady could still be in his life. Of course, that had to wait until after the divorce, as he couldn't stay married to a woman who'd been involved in a kidnapping and baby swap.

***

To tie up loose ends, the body in Jeffery's grave was exhumed and his DNA was tested, and it came as no surprised that it showed he was the son of Mr. and Mrs. McWilliams. When Darrell told Stockwell, he didn't seem surprised to learn the child that was buried in Jeffery Ashby's grave was his son.

Wanting his child, Stockwell arranged for the boy's body to be brought back to St. Louis and be buried where he belonged. Once the baby arrived, he and Angela had a small memorial for him, with their family and some of their friends in attendance.

Angela felt uncomfortable, as she could feel the guests' disapproving stares as their minister preformed the service, as they were all aware of the situation regarding their son's death and switch. Stockwell sat next to her, but they weren't touching, as he still hadn't forgiven her for her error in judgment. She knew after the service, he would return to the hotel he'd been staying at, as he'd already informed her of their pending divorce.

***

Christa hated what she had done to Stockwell and his wife, but what choice did she have, as she wasn't willing to give up her child just so they could have one. Not wanting to bring any more pain to Stockwell than she'd already had, she quit her job and moved back to Kansas City into the home she once shared with her husband.

When the child once known as Brady McWilliams was returned to Christa, she thought the worse was over, but she soon realized that she had a different problem on her hands. Even though Brady, now Jeffery, was her child, the infant couldn't understand why he was away from the only mommy and daddy he'd ever known.

Luckily, after Christa had been back in Kansas City for a week, she noticed the baby was crying less often now, and she assumed he was accepting her as his caregiver. Even so, she knew he was still missing the two people who he thought of as his parents. It's a good thing that he was too young to remember what had happened to him.

***

Since the detective had proof Christa Ashby's child had been stolen, he knew it was time to call in the good doctor and get his side of the story. He went to the man's home and told him he needed to come in for questioning.

Even though Cary Werden knew what this was regarding, he still asked why they wanted to talk to him. The police detective informed him it was regarding a patient of his.

"Dr. Werden, could you please explain what happen on the night Christa Ashby's child was born," Darrell asked him.

"Not much to tell," Cary replied, trying hard not to look nervous about being at the police station. Since it had been over five months since the baby switch, he was sure the police didn't know what he'd done with the woman's infant.

"Walk us through the delivery and his death."

"When the little boy was born, he was greatly deformed. When I'd realized the child would probably die, my wife gave Mrs. Ashby a shot of a strong sedative, as we didn't think she was ready for the news after losing her husband not that long ago."

"I see," said Darrell as he wrote in his notebook.

"I don't understand why months after the fact, I'm here talking about the birth and death of Christa Ashby's infant."

"I'll explain that in a moment. Could you tell me why you were taking care of patients in Kansas City when your office is here in St. Louis? Is that something doctors often do?"

As soon as the detective asked that question, Cary knew he was in deep trouble. He just stared at the detective, unsure if he could lie well enough to get out of this situation.

"Doctor, is there a problem?" Darrell asked, knowing full well, there was.

"No, it's just been awhile and I'm trying to remember the two cases," he said, trying to stall so he could come up with a feasible story.

"Do you want me to refresh your memory?"

"No, that won't be necessary." Cary's mind raced to find a story to tell him, as he didn't want to give him Lloyd's name, not unless he absolutely had to that is. "If I remember correctly, I was asked to consult on Mrs. Ashby's case as her doctors were aware of the baby's defect."

"I see. Now I want you to tell me why you told Mrs. McWilliams her child was going to be deformed, but not Mrs. Ashby?"

Cary was in full panic as this was a tricky question. "Like I said before, I didn't think Mrs. Ashby was mentally strong enough to handle such news after losing her husband such a short time earlier."

"So how come when I saw Mrs. McWilliams' child, he wasn't deformed?"

Damn! If he didn't come up with a good reply, he would be in a load of trouble. Out of the blue, a great idea came to him and he quickly acted on it. "It wasn't until after her child was born that I realized that I had somehow mixed up Mrs. McWilliams's chart with Mrs. Ashby."

"Another good answer. Is that something that happens often?"

"No, but when the charts had fallen off my desk, I mistakenly put the information back in the wrong folders without realizing it."

"This next question is going to be a bit tougher. Since DNA doesn't lie, it's physically impossible for the McWilliams' biological child to have Christa Ashby's DNA. So can you explain how come Brady McWilliams' DNA matches Mrs. Ashby, but neither of the McWilliams? Is that something that can happen, or did you mix the babies up as well?" Darrell smiled a knowing grin at him, as he couldn't wait for the good doctor to try and explain this dilemma.

"I want my lawyer," Cary Werden said, knowing he wasn't going to be able to talk his way out of this mess.

"Of course you do."

***

Lloyd was surprised when he was handed the subpoena to appear in court. Luckily, he was alone when he'd opened the envelope and learned he was being called to court regarding Dr. Werden. Since it didn't mention anything more than that, he knew it had to do with his daughter-in-law and the baby he had the good doctor place in someone else's home.

He contacted his lawyer Walt Utt, to check into the matter. When Walt got back to him, Lloyd wasn't at all surprised to be told that the good doctor had informed the police that he'd had paid him to switch his daughter-in-law's healthy baby with someone's deceased infant.

The case was then given a court date for prosecution of those involved with the kidnapping and illegal placement of Jeffery Ashby into the

McWilliams' home. The local media caught wind of the kidnapping her father-in-law had arranged and soon the whole country was aware of Christa Ashby and the story of the switched babies. Everyone was anxiously waiting for the court proceeding to start, and once again, there were many people hoping Judge James wouldn't be the presiding judge.

***

The day before the court proceedings were to start, Christa had just put Jeffery down for the night when the phone rang. She hurried to it before the sound would wake the baby. "Hello?"

"Christa, Stockwell here."

Fear filled her, as she didn't know what to say to him. She wondered how he got her number and why he was calling.

"You're probably wondering why I'm calling?"

"Yes," she said nervously as she couldn't see anything good coming out of this phone call.

"I want you to know that I've left Angela for what she did to all of us."

Christa wasn't sure why he was telling her this, as it only caused her more pain. "I'm sorry."

"I want to move to Kansas City so I can be in my son's life."

Christa was speechless, as no matter what she said, it would be the wrong thing to say.

"Aren't you going to speak to me?" he asked hatefully.

"Stockwell, you shouldn't punish your wife for what happened."

"You're kidding right?" he asked angrily.

"She didn't know the child had been kidnapped, only that an infant was available for adoption."

"She lied to me," he shouted at her.

"Yes, what she did was wrong, but her heart was in the right place as she wanted to protect you from the loss of your son."

"You sound like you're defending her. How can you do that after what she'd done to you?"

"No one knows what they'd do until they're in a similar situation."

"Are you saying you would have lied to your husband that your son wasn't going to survive his birth and then replace him with someone else's infant?"

Tears filled her eyes. "No, I wouldn't have done that. I'm saying that if you love your wife, you should forgive her, and try for another child."

"I don't want another child; I want the one you have."

"Stockwell, that isn't going to happen as he isn't your son any longer, he's mine."

"He would if you let me be in his life. He has to be missing Angela and me terribly. Don't you think it would be easier on him if one of us were still in his life? If you and I were married, then he would still be my son," he sobbed.

"Stockwell, don't do this to yourself or to me."

"You? You got what you wanted," he hollered.

"Really," she screamed back. "The man I loved is dead and for five months I hadn't any idea if I would ever see my son again. You still have the woman you love, forgive her and move on."

"Will you think about letting me see Brady?" he asked softly, hoping to get back into her good graces.

"His name is Jeffery, and right now I don't think it would be good on anyone for you to see him."

"You're changing his name?" he was shocked.

"Yes, I am."

"Why?" He couldn't understand why she would do that to the boy.

"Because that's his name. Stockwell, please don't call me again. Good-bye," she said gently, and then hung up the phone. She rested her head down on the table and let the tears come, as she thought getting her son back was going to be so wonderful.

But now, she knew that in doing so, she'd hurt three innocent people, one of them who was too young to understand what was happening and why his parents were gone. Was all the pain those blameless ones had to suffer been worth it?

CHAPTER FOURTEEN

Six months earlier

Harrison Ashby had finished his investigation, and now all the information was in the hands of FBI. With his job was over, he decided he would take a break and go fishing. Christa would be okay a few days alone as the baby wasn't due for another month. Not wanting to go alone, he invited several of his college buddies to meet him in Southern Missouri and spend a week together fishing and getting caught up on each other's lives.

After spending seven days fishing with his old school friends, it was time to return to the real world and the wife he loved. His Kia Rio was packed with all his fishing gear, he'd already said good-bye to the guys, and as soon as he ate his breakfast bar, he would be ready to start for home.

Just as he was about to get in his car, he heard someone called his name. When he looked towards the voice, he saw Darby Whieldon racing toward him.

"What's up?"

"My car refused to start. Can you give me a lift home?" Darby asked. He knew it wouldn't be a problem, because his good friend lived just twenty houses down from his home. The two men had driven separately as Darby had joined them after he finished a business meeting.

"Sure, but what about your car? Are you just going to leave it at the camp ground?"

"I've called a tow truck and they're coming for it. When it's fixed, Sue and I will come pick it up."

"I must warn you, my air conditioner isn't working?"

Darby didn't like the idea of driving hundreds of miles in a car without air conditioning, as the summer heat was already beating down on them, but what other choice did he have but to go with it? "I guess I won't melt."

"Do you want to take your fishing gear with you?"

“No, I’m leaving it with the car.”

“Okay, get in and we’ll get going.”

Darby unaware his phone had fallen out of his pocket, he walked to Harrison’s car. The two got into the car and started towards home, and when the sun reached its highest peak, the temperature in car became almost unbearable. Since it was so hot, and they still had over a hundred miles to travel, they decided to stop just outside of Boonville to take a quick dip in the pond they knew about.

Harrison took the exit to the pond, and once the car had stopped, the two men jumped out and ran for the water, racing like two ten-year olds. When they reached the water’s edge, they quickly stripped down to their underwear, throwing their clothes in every which direction, not even bothering to watch where their belongings landed.

Later when Darby got out, without thinking what he was doing, he reached for the pair of jeans that were next to his tee shirt, and so when Harrison exited the water, he dressed in the clothes that were left. Since the brand of their jeans and the size were the same, the two men were unaware they had on each other’s pants.

When Darby offered to drive home, Harrison accepted. Everything was going just fine until Darby tried to slow down when they came to a sharp curve. When the car didn't respond, Darby quickly realizing the brakes were out, he tried to keep control of the car, but at seventy miles an hour, he wasn't successful and the car left the road.

Darby quickly turned the wheel to get the car back on the highway, but the car wouldn't respond, as the car's steeling had given out as well. They both screamed when they saw they were going to hit a very large tree.

When the car made contact with it, Darby was thrown through the windshield, as he hadn't put on his seat belt. The impact caused Harrison's tackle box to fly forward from the back seat and hit him in the head, knocking him unconscious.

When Harrison woke an hour later, he was confused as to what had happened. Seeing the hole in the windshield and the hood of the car up against the tree, he realized they'd been in an accident. When he looked over at the driver seat for Darby, and saw that he wasn't there, he knew he must have gone through the windshield.

"Darby, are you okay?" he called, but he didn't receive an answer. Harrison tried to open his door, finding it stuck; he hit it with his shoulder. "Ouch!" he screamed, as the movement had caused his head to pound more than it already did. Deciding to try the driver's side door, he crawled over the gearshift into the driver's seat and the door opened on the first try.

When he stepped out of the car, and saw Darby's body lying up against the tree, he rushed over to him, knelt down beside him, and carefully turned him over. When he saw his friend's face, or what was left of it, he gasped out loud, as the tree had demolished his friend's boyish good looks.

"Oh Darby, I'm so sorry." He didn't know why he was apologizing, other than the fact; they'd been in his car.

When Harrison stood, he wobbled a bit before he regained his balance. He put his hand up to his head where it was throbbing and when he brought his hand back, he wasn't surprised to see there was blood on it.

He wiped the blood onto his tee shirt, and then took it off, bunched it up in a ball, and put it against his head to help stop the bleeding. As he rested his head against the tee shirt, he reached into his pocket with his other hand to get his cell phone. When all he pulled out was a handful of change, he was confused, as he didn't understand where his phone could have gone.

He looked at his friend. "I've lost my phone, so I have to go for help. It may take me awhile to find anyone, so you'll have to be patient with me."

He hurt everywhere, but he had to ignore the pain, as he needed to find help for his friend. Unaware of his internal bleeding, Harrison took off down the country road without realizing it was already too late to help Darby.

Harrison walked until he couldn't walk any further, as his physical condition was taking its toll on him. He decided to sit down and rest for a bit before continuing, but as he started to lower his body, he passed out. As he fell to the ground, his body rolled towards the side of an embankment, and then it disappeared over the edge. He rolled over the rough terrain to the bottom of the hill, with his body stopping with him lying on his side.

When a teenager came across Harrison's body twenty minutes later, he thought the man was dead. Deciding a dead man wouldn't need his wallet, the young boy decided to help himself to it. Just as his hand grabbed the wallet in the man's back pocket, a hand reached out and grabbed hold of his wrist.

The teenager thinking the man's ghost had hold of him, screamed, and took off like a bat out of hell with the wallet tightly grasped in his fist. When the boy finally quit running and opened the wallet, he gasped at all the cash that was in it. Without even bothering to count it, he folded it in half, stuck it in his front pant pocket and threw the wallet towards the bushes. He simply walked away, never reporting the injured man as he didn't want to return the money he'd stolen.

***

A farmer and his family driving home noticed a vehicle up against a tree, so he slowed down, stopping as close as he could. He told his family to stay put, then he got out and stepped toward the car.

When he saw the man's body, he ran forward to check on him. The man appeared to be dead, but knowing he had to be sure, the farmer knelt down next to him and put his finger on the man's neck. When he couldn't find a pulse, he looked down at this chest to check for any movement, but there wasn't any. He stood, pulled out his cell phone, and called the sheriff's department to report the accident.

It wasn't long before the authorities arrived; they checked for identification and found the man was Harrison Ashby from Kansas City. And since his face had been destroyed when it collided with the tree, no one even thought to question his identity. They then called the Kansas City Police to ask them to inform the family about Harrison's death.

***

Meanwhile, just down the street from Christa's home, Sue Whieldon was watching the clock as she waited for her husband's return. When Darby was two hours late, she knew something was wrong and tried his cell phone. When he didn't answer, she called the police, but they couldn't help her until her husband had been missing for at least 24 hours. Deciding she couldn't wait that long, she called Harrison's home to see if he knew anything about Darby.

When she reached Christa, Sue was shocked to hear that Harrison had been killed in a car accident on his way home. And since there had been only Harrison's stuff in the car, Christa didn't have any idea the two men had been together at the time of the accident, nor the fact it had been her friend's husband who had been killed, not hers

After Christa told her father-in-law about Harrison's death, she told him that she had been married to his son, and was expecting his child next month. Lloyd said she was lying and not to call him again because she wouldn't be getting a single dime from him and then simply hung up.

***

When Harrison was found a day later, he was alive. He had internal injuries and additional head trauma from his fall down the hill; he was also extremely dehydrated from being without water for so many hours.

He was rushed by helicopter to the nearest hospital where surgery was performed to repair the damage to his left kidney and fluids were given for the dehydration. Luckily, he had been in the shade the whole time; otherwise, he would have had severe burns on his face, arms and legs as well. They thought he would make a full recovery, but after the surgery, he remained in a coma.

The hospital personnel tried to find out who he was, but without any form of ID on him, they came up empty. The police were called, but no one matching his description had been reported missing anywhere in the entire country. A Darby Whieldon, a Kansas City man, had been report missing, but he didn't match the description of their John Doe, they had the Intensive Care Unit. The authorities never thought the two situations were related, so Sue Whieldon was still unaware her husband had been the one killed, and not Harrison.

When Harrison had been at the hospital for a week, he was sent to a nursing home, as they weren't for sure if he would ever regain consciousness. Day after day passed until thirty days had gone by since the accident, and on the thirty-first day, he started regaining consciousness. But even then, he was in and out of it most of the time.

On the fortieth day, Harrison opened his eyes and looked directly into the eyes of a young aid; the girl startled to see him awake, let out a squeal, and ran out of the room. When the charge nurse arrived, she found Harrison trying to get out of bed and rushed to his side.

"Sir, you've been ill, please you must stay in bed."

His sad eyes looked at the nurse. "Who am I?"

"Damn!" she exclaimed.

Harrison gave her a perplexed look.

"I'm sorry. We were hoping that when you woke you would be able to tell us who you were."

"Don't you know?"

"You came in without any form of ID." She then told him all she knew about him, which wasn't much.

***

Even though Harrison still didn't know who he was, a week later he was released from the nursing home. Becca Torres, a young woman who worked part time at the nursing home, hoping someday Harrison would be hers, found a studio apartment for him.

Harrison had been tested to see what kind of job he would be good at, and the results showed he had an aptitude for numbers. And since Becca's brother was the president of the accounting firm where she worked full time, she found him a job as well.

Since Harrison didn't remember his name, he had asked Becca to give him one so people had something to call him by for now. So she had open the white pages at random, closed her eyes, and then put her finger down on the page. When she opened her eyes and looked down, she laughed, as the name was Bunny Abbott. She tried a second time, and this time the name was Montgomery Nye. Since he couldn't use the man's first and last name, Becca gave him her last name, telling him he could be a long lost relative, which made him laugh, as he was definitely lost. And so Montgomery Torres was created.

A bond was made between the two, one that Becca would like to see change to one of a romantic nature, but since he was wearing a wedding ring, Harrison refused to let the relationship develop into anything other than being friends.

The first few months were frustrating for Harrison, for no matter how hard he tried, he couldn't remember who he was or where he was from. But by the time of the fifth month since his accident rolled around, he had started having a faint memory of a beautiful woman. He was frustrated, as the harder he tried to put a name to the face, the more it disappeared.

Seeing Addison, one of his coworkers, with a baby name book, he had the great inspiration and so he hurried over to her. "Addison, may I borrow your baby book?"

She gave him a strange look. "Of course, but why do you want it?"

"I thought maybe if I looked at all the names, I might recognize my wife's name, and once I knew hers, maybe mine would come to me."

Addison was touched by the hopefully look on his face, so she didn't tell him she doubted it would do any good, as the book had over five thousand names. "Sure." She handed him the book. "Can I help in any way?"

"Thanks, but this is something I have to do alone."

Addison nodded, wishing her husband would look at her the way Harrison did at the thought of remembering his wife's name.

Harrison took the book, then returned to his office and shut the door. He sat down at his desk and opened the first page. Starting with the letter A, he began saying each name out loud. When none of those names sounded familiar, he started with the next letter, and only knowing his wife's name could be Yvonne, kept him from giving up.

He started on the next letter. "Chelsey, Cheryl, Cheyenne, Chloe, Chris," he stopped, as the name Chris seemed to mean something, but it didn't feel right. "Chrissa, Chrissy," he said, saying each one of them slowly. The names seemed to jog his memory, but something was still off, so he went on to the next name.

"Christa," he said, and a faint tingle went up his arm. "Christa," he repeated. "This is my wife, Christa," he said as a smile covered his face, as he was positive his wife's name was Christa.

Now all he had to do was figure out his own name. He started flipping through the pages until he came to the letter A under the boys' names, but before he could say the first name, Becca knocked on the door.

"Are you coming to the monthly meeting?" Becca asked as she opened his door.

Harrison looked down at his watch, and seeing the time, he was surprised to see how late it was. "Becca, I'm sorry. I sort of lost track of the time."

"No, problem, the sandwiched have just arrived."

Harrison stood and joined her at the door. "I think getting together to discuss any problems we're having with our work is a great team building activity."

"Thanks," she said, then turned and started to the kitchen where the meeting was being held.

When the two entered the room, George and Addison were discussing from what Harrison could determine something out of the newspaper as George had one in his hand.

"I can't believe the man could steal a child and get away with it just because he has money. If that man get off, then that just shows judges can be bought."

George's words seemed to ring a bell in Harrison's head, but he didn't know what it could possible mean. "What are you two talking about?" he asked as he picked up the box that held his requested sandwich and chips in it.

George threw the paper down in front of Harrison. "Here read it for yourself."

Harrison picked up the paper, and as soon as he saw the woman's picture on the page, he gasped. Tears began running down his cheeks as his life came rushing back to him. Thinking of Christa and the love they shared, a warm glow of love filled his chest.

He quickly read the story, and became furious when he saw what his father had done to his wife and child.

"Montgomery, are you okay?" George asked, as he was concerned why the article had upset him so much.

"My name is Harrison Ashby, and this is my wife," he said as he put the paper back down on the counter. He looked up at his friends. "My wife thinks I'm dead, I have to go home to her. I have to be there when court resumes today."

The room was filled with a lot of discussion, but Harrison didn't have time to talk. He told them he would be back after he took care of this matter to finish up any business he still had here.

Becca sadly watched him leave the room, as she now knew for sure that he wouldn't ever be hers.

***

The family had been devastated when they learned that Judge James was the judge presiding over Christa's case against Lloyd Ashby. They tried to get him removed, but the motion had been denied, as they didn't have a good reason to have him dismissed.

When the trial started, Lloyd was the first one called to the witness stand.

"Mr. Ashby, I have a picture here that I'd like you to look at. Can you tell me if you've ever seen it before?" Patrick Nelson, Christa's lawyer asked Lloyd.

Not only was Lloyd surprised to be call as the first witness, he was confused why the man wanted him to look at some damn photo. He took the picture, furious at being accused of being involved in the switching of Christa's child with another infant, something this lowly lawyer couldn't prove as he'd covered his tracks well.

Though the doctor was claiming he was involved, Cary didn't have any proof Lloyd had actually hired him for the crime. Any money that had traded hands had been from Lloyd's private stash of hundred dollar bills, and without any paper trail to connect him to the crime; it was the doctor's word against his.

"It's a picture of my son, but I don't remember ever seeing it before. What does it have to do with this case?" he demanded.

"This isn't a picture of your son, but that of Jeffery Ashby, your grandson. He's the child you had switched with a deceased child because you didn't think Christa was having your grandchild."

Lloyd's face suddenly lost all its color. Had Christa been telling the truth about giving birth to Harrison's child? If so, he had really screw things up with what he'd done. "I don't know what you are talking about. I didn't have anything to do with what Dr. Werden did. Besides, I don't even know the doctor."

"If this is true, would you care to explain why you asked Christa to use Dr. Werden?"

"A friend recommended him to me."

"That isn't what Dr. Werden tells us. He said the two of you went to college together."

"I don't care what he's been saying, it's all lies."

"Maybe some of them are lies, but we have documented proof that not only did the two of you had several classes together, but you and Cary Werden were roommates for the four years you attended college."

He frowned as he didn't know how to respond to his comment, as it was all true. To throw the lawyer off that track he went in a different direction. "I would never give away my son's child, so I hadn't any reason to hire him."

"Not even when you thought Christa Ashby was lying about having Harrison's child?" Patrick turned towards the jury. "We have DNA proof that the child that has been living in the McWillams' home for the past five months is Harrison and Christa Ashby's child." He quickly turned around to look at Lloyd. "Do you want to explain why you had the good doctor exchange your son's child with another couple's dead baby?"

"I'm thrilled to see my grandchild is alive, but as I told you, I didn't have anything to do with what Dr. Werden did. He's lying in order to save his own butt."

"And why would he tell us such a lie? Maybe because it isn't a lie, but the actions of a man paid to commit a crime for an old buddy from college."

When Walt Utt saw he was about to lose his case, he call for a lunch break, as it was already after one. The judge then called for a two-hour lunch break, saying they would resume court at three. Walt leaned over to Lloyd to discuss their strategy, but he didn't think it would do any good for his client.

***

When court resumed, it was Cary Werden's turn to tell his side of the story. Since he had made a deal with the police to save his butt, he spilled his guts on Lloyd's crime and his part in it. He looked over at

Christa and told her how very sorry for causing her to lose her son.

An hour later, the jury left the room to decide Lloyd's fate, and after deliberating for less than fifteen minutes, the jury returned to the courtroom. Everyone in the room watched as they took their seat in the jury box, whispering about what the verdict was going to be.

Judge James pounded his mallet for silence. "Silence in the courtroom."

The jury foreman stood. "We the people of the jury find Lloyd Ashby guilty of all charges."

Everyone in the room was thrilled with the jury's guilty verdict, but then the judge did something no one expected, that is, except Lloyd.

"I'm sorry, but I don't agree with your finding," Judge James stated loud enough for everyone in the room to hear him.

The entire courtroom went silent.

"I don't think Mr. Ashby is guilty of any crime, but has been falsely accused by Dr. Werden in order to save his own skin, therefore Lloyd Ashby is free to...," he started, raising his mallet in the air.

"Judge James, I always wondered if my father could buy you off, and now I know the answer," Harrison stated coldly. Then he looked around the room, "as well as every person in this room."

Hearing her husband's voice, Christa turned. Expecting to see someone who just happened to sound like her Harrison, she was speechless when she saw him standing at the back of the courtroom.

Judge James was shocked to see Harrison before him, as he was supposed to be dead, as he had paid a great deal of money to see that he never saw another day. If his body wasn't the one found with his car, then whose body had been found with Harrison's car?

"I bet you're shocked to see me standing here before you?" Harrison asked, as he knew the judge was the reason his good friend was dead.

"I'm in charge here, I have the final word regarding if Lloyd Ashby is guilty or not." He was furious by this man's accusation.

"You may think you have the authority, but you're wrong. If you think my father will save your job, I wouldn't bet on it," Harrison uttered, and then laughed. "Especially when he learns you hired a hit man to kill me. It was a tragic accident, as a good friend of mine was killed in my place," he said. "His face was destroyed to the point he wasn't even recognizable."

When he sense Christa's eyes on him, he wanted to hurry to where she stood and pulled her into his arms, but he had to remain where he was and finish what he'd started.

"My wife has suffered enough at the hands of my father. He conspired with the doctor to steal her child away, not caring how she would survive losing a husband and a child in such a short time span."

"That's enough out of you," Judge James yelled as he pounded his mallet on his desk.

"No, your Honor, it isn't. You are under arrest not only for taking bribes to change verdicts of guilty parties, but also in the murder of Amy Thompson."

Judge James' face turned white.

"You remember her don't you, your Honor. Amy was the prostitute that you were involved with and had killed because she threatened to expose you. You are also under arrest for the murder of Darby Whieldon. But before they take you away, I think you need fix the ruling on Lloyd Ashby."

When the police surrounded the judge, he knew he wasn't going to be able to get out of this mess. "I agree with the jury's verdict. Lloyd Ashby is to serve twenty-five years in prison for the kidnapping of Jeffery Ashby. He's to be taken into custody and begin serving his sentence immediately."

Harrison turned to his father. "Any last words, Father."

Tears began to form in the older man's eyes. "I was afraid she would try to bleed me dry, while claiming another man's child as your heir." He turned to Christa. "I'm sorry."

When his father and the judge were taken away and the courtroom started emptying, he rushed to his wife and pulled her into his arms.

"Harrison, I don't understand. Why was Darby driving your car?" she asked after the breathtaking kiss from her husband.

"Darby's car broke down and I was taking him home," he said, and then he explained everything that happened from that day until this moment.

"So you're saying you've had amnesia for the six months and only gotten your memory back earlier today?"

"Yes," he said. "I'm sorry you suffered so much because of my father and Judge James, but now it's all over and we can be the family we're meant to be."

***

Harrison went to Sue's home to inform her of her husband's death. She was sadden by the news, but relieved finally to know what happened to him. Instead of digging up Darby's body and moving him to another plot, Harrison asked Sue if they could simply change the marker to Darby's name. Hating the thought of digging up her husband's final resting place, she agreed. After that was done, they had a small memorial service for Darby Whieldon.

CHAPTER FIFTEEN

Unbeknown to his sisters, Grayson had taken summer classes, so he was able to graduate a long side his sisters. He knew if he wanted to continue to eat and have utilities, he had to find a job and quickly. Grayson thought it would take him months to find a job that would pay well, so he was prepared for the long wait. Two days after starting his search, a great job practically fell in his lap, as he'd been hired as the *Director-in-Charge* at a local publishing firm company.

When Jayna and Monroe announced to the family that they had secretly gotten married, Grayson had moved back to the family place to give the newlyweds some privacy. When Monroe had been killed, he thought about moving back to be close to Jayna, but before he could, she'd up and married Colin. He wasn't surprised by the secretive wedding, as he been aware how Colin felt about sister from when they were kids.

When Grayson's twenty-first birthday arrived, and they received their father's insurance money, the first thing Grayson did was buy back the family place from Albert. Not wanting to use any more of his inheritance than he had already had, he put the rest away in the bank for *a rainy day.*

With a good salary now coming in, he decided it was time ask Sharron O'Bannon, his college sweetheart to marry him. They didn't have a big flashy wedding, as Grayson wanted to keep the cost down to save money, so just their family and a few friends attended the ceremony.

A few months later when the company he worked for went up for sale, he decided it was *a rainy day*, and without even talking it over with his wife, he took the money out of savings and bought the company. It wasn't until he changed the name to *Sims Publishing Company* did she realized what he'd done.

So furious at him for spending their money without her consulting her about it, Sharron went out to a bar, where she happened to run into her old boyfriend, Dale Starke. After having too much to drink, she went to a motel room with him, where she had unprotected sex with him. Of course, she couldn't ever tell Grayson what she'd done, but her rebellion brought her a great deal of satisfaction just the same. That is until she missed her next period.

Grayson thought his life was going great, not only were his sisters both blissfully married with little boys, but he too was happily married, or so he thought. The next day he learned everything wasn't rosy in his marriage as he assumed.

"Grayson, I'm pregnant," Sharron, his wife of six months, told him nervously.

"That's a surprise," he responded tensely, as he realized something wasn't right here. They'd always used condoms when they made love, so how come she was pregnant and why was she acting so nervous. "Is there more you want to tell me?" he asked, hoping she would tell him something that would make him feel better about her announcement.

"You know, don't you?" Sharron asked tearfully, as her guilty conscience had been bothering her ever since that night she'd stepped out on her husband.

Grayson just stared at her as he was unsure how to answer her. There was something going on here, and maybe if he played his cards just right, she might spill the beans that would enlighten him what he needed to know. "I have my suspicions," he said, hoping the truth would come out.

She put her hands up to her face and started crying. "I'm so sorry. I never meant for you to find out what I did."

Grayson remained quiet, hoping she would continue with her confession.

Finally, she removed her hands from her face, but didn't look at him. "I met Dale one night at a bar. We started flirting, and the next thing I knew, we were at the motel across the street doing *the nasty*. Since protection was the last thing on my mind, I got pregnant that night."

When Sharron's words entered his brain, Grayson felt as if his world had been torn from beneath him. "Dale, your ex-boyfriend?" he asked, shocked she would have anything to do with him since he was the one who wanted the breakup.

"Yes."

"So you're saying he's the father."

“Probably,” she replied as she looked up at him.

“How could you do that to our marriage?” he asked softly, sadden that she’d been unfaithful.

“I was angry at you for buying the publishing company you worked for without even talking it over with me. I went to a bar to drown my sorrows, and I got drunk and ended up making the biggest mistake of my life.”

“So you’re saying all this is my fault?” he asked, shocked at the thought she blamed him.

“No, of course not. I’m explaining why I went to the bar in the first place.”

“I’m sorry I didn’t tell you about what I was planning on doing. I guess it’s because I’m still not used to talking to someone before I make a decision regarding my life. You’re right I should have talked it over with you, and for that, I’m sorry.

“Knowing about your inheritance, I thought once you received it, we would start living the good life.”

For a split second, he could only stare at her. “You’re saying you married me only because of my inheritance?”

Sharron had to be careful how she answered, as Grayson wasn’t a stupid man. If she answered incorrectly, she would find herself on the streets before she could blink, but if she said the right things, maybe he would forgive her and they could raise this baby together. "No, of course not."

Grayson wasn't so sure, and the more he thought of it, he realized that was exactly what she'd done. "Did you even love me?" he asked tearful, his heart breaking at learning the truth about his marriage.

Figuring she still had chance with him, she told him what she thought he wanted to hear. "Of course I have feelings for you; otherwise I wouldn't have married you."

"Did you tell Dale about the baby?"

"I told him, but he doesn't want the baby," Sharron said as she looked down at her hands. What she didn't tell her husband was what Dale had called her when he learned that he'd slept with a married woman. Since he'd had broken all ties with her when he'd moved away, he wasn't aware that she'd gotten married, until the morning after they had sex.

"Do you still have feelings for Dale? And I want an honest answer," he demanded coldly.

"No, I just like the attention he gave me. He always spent a great deal of money on me while we were dating, and I miss someone buying me things I wanted, so that's why I took him up on the drinks."

Grayson was torn what to do as he loved his wife, but he didn't think he could ever trust her again. He didn't want a woman who married him for his money nor care if she cheated on her wedding vows. "Since you seem to love money more than you do me, I think it would be best if we file for divorce and go our separate ways."

Her heart sank at his statement. "Grayson, I hate to tell you this, but it isn't that simple."

"What do you mean?" he asked angrily.

"You can't get a divorce while the wife's pregnant, so we'll have to wait until after the baby's born before proceeding with it." Sharron didn't know if that was true, but if they were living together, maybe she could get him to change his mind about the divorce.

"Fine. Go live with your brother or find a place of your own. I don't care where you live, but it isn't going to be here."

"Grayson, be reasonable," she begged.

"Reasonable," he screamed at her. "You tell me you've been unfaithful with an old boyfriend and probably pregnant with his child, and yet you expect me to allow you to stay here just because your lover doesn't want the baby?" He took in a deep breath. "Pack your bags and get out of here immediately, or I'll start throwing your belongings out into the yard."

"Fine, I you're going to be like that, then I'll just pack and get out of your life." She left the room and headed towards their bedroom.

He followed her, as he wanted to make sure she didn't pack any items that didn't belong to her. After she packed some of her clothes, she told him she would be back tomorrow to get the rest of her stuff.

"Call me when the baby comes," Grayson said as she marched to her car. "No matter if the child is mine or not, I'm ending this marriage."

Once she was out of sight, he went to the computer, clicked on the Internet, and went to *Ask.com* and typed in '*Can you get a divorce in Missouri when the wife's pregnant?*'

Several links popped up and he clicked on one with the heading *Divorcing While Pregnant Laws in Missouri* and as he read, a smile appeared on his face. Sharron hadn't been completely correct by her statement as the article said the pregnancy can often delay divorce, but depending on certain factors, it could be finalized before the baby came.

As he read on, he was greatly relieved to learn that he wouldn't have to pay child support for a child that wasn't his, but spousal support may be ordered. That didn't bother him, as that was something he could fight and if he did happened to lose, it was something he could live with.

When he was finished with the Internet, he called to make an appointment with Colin, as he knew his brother-in-law wouldn't steer him in the wrong direction. At their meeting, Colin told him he was sorry that his marriage was ending and asked if either of his sisters knew what was going on in his life. Grayson replied that they didn't, but he would call them later, but for now, he wanted Colin to file the divorce papers.

Colin suggested Grayson waited until after the baby was born and he knew positively that he wasn't the child's father before proceeding. He informed Grayson that in cases like his, some judges demanded the husband pay child support, even if the child wasn't his, just to be spiteful. Since Grayson didn't want to pay for a child that wasn't his, he agreed to wait. Colin said he would get the paperwork ready, and after the child's birth and they knew for sure Grayson wasn't the father of Sharron's baby, he would file the divorce papers.

***

Meanwhile, Sharron was at her brother's home, asking Chuck O'Bannon if she could move in with him. When her brother asked why she wanted to live with him, she told him that Grayson was divorcing her, leaving out the fact that she had married him for his money and was probably pregnant with her ex-boyfriend's child.

Chuck had kept his cool, but when Sharron went to her car to bring in her stuff, he let out an explosive cuss word. He decided the first thing tomorrow, he was going to Grayson's office and beat the man to a bloody pulp, as he had to pay for what he'd done to his sister.

***

Grayson and one of his editors, Lisa Tidwell were in his office going over some of the novels that were so horrible they were unsellable. It was now Lisa's job to send them a letter stating their novels had been rejected and the reasons why. Of course she wouldn't tell them how awful their manuscripts were, only that they wouldn't be publishing it.

They had just finished up when the office door flew open and Chuck stormed in, so startled at the interruption, Lisa screamed, as the man looked angry enough to kill someone.

Grayson quickly stood and started towards Chuck. "Chuck, you can't just come barging into my office like this."

Chuck looked over at the attractive woman, who had a petrified expression on her face. "If you don't want your employee to see what I'm about to do to your face, I suggest she leaves the room," he said as each of his hands formed a fist.

Grayson looked over at Lisa. "Why don't you go back to your office and contact the authors we discussed earlier."

Her eyes wide looked back at him in horror at the thought of Grayson being beaten up. "You want me to call someone?"

"No, I'll be fine. Please shut the door on your way out."

After Lisa had left the room, shutting the door behind her, Grayson faced his brother-in-law. "I'm guessing you're here because of your sister."

"You think?" he asked coldly. "You want to explain why you kicked your wife out of your home."

"I can, but I think Sharron should be the one to tell you the reason why."

"Why can't you be a man and just tell me?" he demand.

"Because you won't like it what I have to say, is why."

"Tell me anyway," he stated as his cold eyes stared at Grayson.

"Fine! She doesn't love me and only married me for my inheritance. Would you want to stay married to someone who only married you for your money?"

Chuck was speechless for a moment as his anger turned to disappointment. "Are you sure?" he inquired softly.

"She told me herself."

"I guess I can't blame you for kicking her out. I'm sorry for storming in here and threatening you."

"I would do the same thing if it was my sister."

"I'm sure you would. I hope the next woman you marry, marries you because she loves you."

"Thanks, me too."

***

As the months passed, Chuck soon became aware of his sister's enlarging belly, and once again, anger filled him. This time when he stormed into Grayson's office, he was alone. "Where's the pretty little thing that was in here the last time I visited?"

"Chuck, what do you what?"

"You knocked up my sister and then threw her out just because she doesn't love you. You can't treat the mother of your child like that. I should kill you for what you have done to my sister."

"Chuck, I beg of you to talk to Sharron, as it isn't my place to tell you."

"I'm not leaving until I get a straight answer."

By Chuck's stance, Grayson knew he meant business. He couldn't tell him what he wanted to know, as Chuck wouldn't take it kindly if he insulted his sister.

"Well?" Chuck demanded loudly.

"You can kill me it you want, but if you want to know why I kicked her out of my home, ask Sharron, as I'm not going to be the one to tell you."

"Fine, have it your way, but if you end up dead, you can't say I didn't warn you."

***

As the months passed, and Grayson didn't hear anything from Sharron or Chuck, he assumed Sharron told her brother who the father was and didn't think any more about it. The day after Sharron's daughter, Anne Marie was born, a DNA test was performed, and when the test results proved Grayson wasn't the child's father, Colin started on the divorce proceedings. Since the child wasn't his, Grayson never came to see the baby or sent any child support for her.

***

When Sharron learned for sure who her daughter's father was, she called Dale and asked if he wanted to see his daughter, as Anne deserved to have her father in her life.

When Dale came to the hospital to see his daughter, Sharron explained to him that she and Grayson were getting a divorce. He told her that since he wanted to be in his daughter's life, maybe they could try again at their relationship.

CHAPTER SIXTEEN

Just before lunch, Grayson handed Lisa several manuscripts, telling her he needed them done by the end of the day. Therefore, instead of joining her coworkers who were going out for lunch, she started working on the manuscript that had the fewest number of pages. As she read it, she found it to be boring; the writing was so horrible that if it had been up to her, she would have thrown the entire story in the trash. But since it wasn't up to her, she continued reading and marking all the errors, and when she finished there were so many red marks on the pages, it wasn't even funny.

When her tummy growled, she decided to grab her lunch from the refrigerator and eat at her desk, and just as she stepped away from her desk, Chuck entered the office. Seeing the place was empty of employees, Chuck went straight into Grayson's office, lifted his right hand, and pointed a gun at him.

Grayson hearing someone entering his office, he looked up. Expecting to see Lisa, he was shaken to see his ex-brother-in-law pointing a gun at him. "Chuck, don't do this," he yelled.

Chuck pulled the trigger repeatedly, shooting Grayson in the chest as he emptied his gun. After Grayson fell to the floor, Chuck turned and stepped out of the office, and came face to face with Lisa. Knowing he couldn't let her call the police, he brought his hands up to her throat and started squeezing.

Lisa dropped her lunch sack, and brought her hands up to his to break his grip, but he was too strong for her. Not knowing what else to do, she moved her hands to his cheeks, and raked her fingernails down the side of his face. She thought he would release her, but instead his grip just tightened and then everything went black.

***

Lisa woke up from her nightmare shaking and gasping for air as if she indeed had been strangled. Feeling something wet on her checks, she put her hand up to her cheeks and was surprised to find tears on them. As she continued to sit there, her nightmare came back to her.

It had all started when Grayson had given her some manuscripts to work on during the weekend, and since she wanted to get the work done as soon as possible, she had started working on them at six this morning so she would have the rest of the weekend to herself.

When she'd finished editing three of the manuscripts, she decided to eat some lunch before beginning on the next one. With her belly satisfied, and the warm sun shining through the window on her, her eyes began getting heavy. Soon her eyes closed and she'd fell asleep, with the red pen still in her hand. Her head dropped downwards, and a second later, she was asleep.

She wasn't sure what had woken her, but she was glad something had. Since her dream had seemed so real, she had to be sure Grayson was okay, so she picked up her cell phone. Just when she thought her call was going to go into his voice mail, he answered the phone.

Grayson had just stepped out of the shower when he heard his cell ringing. After wrapping the towel around his waist, he hurried into his bedroom picked up his phone from the bedside table. Seeing it was Lisa, Grayson almost didn't connect the call, as he was afraid she was calling to rant and rave at him for the stack of manuscripts he'd given her to work on during her day off.

"Are you ready for some more manuscripts?" he asked with a teasing tone, hoping to lighten her mood.

She let out a deep sigh of relief at hearing his voice.

"Lisa, what's wrong? Are you okay?" he quickly asked, as he sensed something had upset her. "Did you get some bad news?"

"I just had a bad dream about you. It was so ghastly; that I just needed to hear your voice to be sure you were unharmed."

Her words touched him more than she could know, as he was falling in love with her and wanted her to be his wife. He hadn't found the nerve to ask her out yet, as he didn't want anything to come between their working together. But in order for her to become his wife; he would eventually have to ask her out. "Can you tell me about the dream?" he asked, as he didn't want her to hang up yet.

"That horrible man, Chuck O'Bannon rushed into the office and shot you several times in the chest. As he exited your office, he ran into me. Not wanting me to go to the police, he started strangling me. Luckily, that's when I woke up. It seemed so real that I couldn't relax until I knew you were alive. Since you're okay, I should let you go."

Grayson was shocked by Lisa's comment, as just last week, Chuck had indeed stormed into Grayson office and threatened to kill him if he didn't start supporting his child. And once again, Grayson told him he needed to talk to his sister. He would have been more than happy to support Anne Marie if she'd been his, but she wasn't, and he had the DNA proof she wasn't his responsibility.

Grayson wondered if Lisa's dream was a premonition of what was going to transpire or simply a freak dream. Since he couldn't take the chance of the shooting happening, he needed to call Sharron and make sure she told her brother that he wasn't the child's father.

"Lisa, don't hang up yet," he said hurriedly, his voice full of his urgency.

"What's wrong?" she asked, as she sensed something was amiss.

"Chuck has threatened my life."

"What?" she cried. "Did he threaten you that day he barged into your office?"

"No, he stopped by last week while everyone was out to lunch."

"Why does he want to hurt you?"

"This isn't something I wanted to talk about on the phone, but I think this is something you need to hear."

"Okay, I'm listening."

"He's angry because I'm not paying child support for my ex-wife's child."

"Oh, my. I can understand why he's angry." She didn't know much about Grayson's ex-wife or their daughter, as he never spoke of them.

"What Chuck doesn't know is that Anne Marie isn't mine." He didn't leave anything out including the fact his wife hadn't ever loved him, marrying him only for his inheritance. He quickly explained about Sharron having an affair with her ex-boyfriend and the DNA test they had done that proved the baby wasn't his.

"Oh Grayson, I'm so sorry."

"Don't worry about any of this as I'm going to make sure Sharron tells her brother the truth about her daughter's father."

***

On Monday afternoon, Grayson went over the manuscripts Lisa had worked on over the weekend. After agreeing with her assessment on the stack, he informed her that in the morning he wanted her to type up the rejection letters. When she was done, she was to have him sign them and then mailed them to the writers.

Grayson said goodnight to her, and as he watched her leave the office, he wished he had the nerve to declare his feelings for her. He had just turned off his computer when the phone rang, thinking it might be important he answered it. "Hello?" he said, then waited for someone to speak.

"I'm looking for a Lisa Tidwell," the male voice said.

Grayson picked up a piece of paper to write on. "I'm sorry but she has left for the day, may I take a message?"

"It's extremely important that I get in touch with her."

"If you leave your name and phone number, I'll make sure she gets the message."

"I'm calling on the behalf of her brother, Ethan VanCamp."

Grayson didn't like sound of this call, not one little bit. "I think you have the wrong Lisa, as she doesn't have a brother."

"I have the right Lisa as I got this number from the lawyer who took care of her parents' estate. She was adopted as a baby, and as far as I know, she doesn't know she has any siblings."

"If you're after money, I can tell you right now that she doesn't have any she can give to this brother."

The man laughed. "No, that's not what he needs from her. You see, Ethan has a rare form of an immune system disease and has been quite ill for the past few months. He's in desperately need of a bone marrow, so all he needs from his sister is her bone marrow and nothing more."

"Where is he now?"

"In the hopes that Lisa would be willing to donate, we transported him to North Kansas City hospital yesterday."

Grayson felt uneasy, as Lisa hadn't ever mentioned that she'd been adopted. "I'll make sure she gets the message, but I can't guarantee that she'll call you back." The man gave Grayson the phone number, but that was all. "And your name?"

"Dennis," he said.

"Well Dennis, do you have a last name?"

"VanCamp," he said softly.

Grayson's eyebrows rose. "So you're related to Ethan?"

Dennis didn't want to tell him, but getting this message to Lisa was too important to play games with her boss. "Yes, I'm his father."

Grayson frowned, as he didn't like how this was going. "I'll give Lisa your message."

"Thank you," Dennis said, even though he didn't think the man would.

As soon as the two men hung up, Grayson took the paper with the man's information and started for Lisa's home, as this was too important to say over the phone.

CHAPTER SEVENTEEN

Lisa stood up when she heard a knock at her front door. When she reached the door, and looked out through the storm door, she was surprised to see Grayson and his troubled expression. Concerned why he was at her home, she quickly opened the door. "Grayson, what's wrong?"

After he walked into the house unsure how to begin, he took hold of her hand. "Did you know you were adopted?"

Lisa smiled. "A matter of fact, I did. The question is how do you know that?"

"I have something to tell you, but I don't want to do it here. Can we sit down first?"

"Sure," she replied, worried that he was here to tell her some bad news.

After they moved to the couch and sat down, Grayson took hold of her hand, but then just looked at her.

"You want to tell me why you asked about my adoption?" Her eyes watched him closely, trying to decide where this conversation was going.

He wondered how what he had to tell her was going to affect her, but since he wouldn't know until he told her, he started to speak. The words came out sounding like a croak, so he quickly cleared his throat, and started again. "A man called me at the office shortly after you left today and said he was calling on behalf of your brother."

Lisa's eyes grew round. "I have a brother?"

"That's what the man said. Did you ever try to find your birth parents?"

"I thought about it after my parents died, but I decided against it."

"Why's that?" he inquired, as he just assume all children of adoption would want to meet their birth parents.

"My birth parents were just two people who created me, nothing more, while my adoptive parents were my Mom and Dad."

Grayson quickly conveyed the conversation he had with Dennis, her brother's adoptive father, telling her how sick her brother was and what they needed from her.

"I want to help him."

He gave her a concerned look. "Is this going to be hard on you seeing a brother you didn't know you had?"

"I'm not sure. Part of me is excited, but the other part is worried he won't like me."

Grayson chuckled. "I don't see that happening."

"I guess I could take a couple days of my vacation and fly to see him." She frowned when she saw Grayson shaking his head. "Why not? You think I shouldn't meet him?"

"Just the opposite, as I think you should meet him, but leaving town isn't necessary."

Her face brightened up. "He lives in the area?"

"No, but he's been transferred here in the hopes you're a match and the transplant could happen immediately. You need to call his father to see if he's up to receiving guests, and if he is, you can go right now."

Lisa took the paper from him and dialed the number to her brother's hospital room.

When Dennis' phone rang, he answered the phone, praying it was Lisa calling him. "Hello?" he answered.

"This is Lisa Tidwell; I'm calling about my brother."

"Lisa, I'm so happy that you called so quickly. I guess your boss explained the situation to you?" He just hoped she wasn't calling to say she didn't want to help.

"Yes, he did."

"I hope you weren't surprised to learn you had been adopted."

"My parents told me when I was about five, but they didn't tell me that I had a brother. Do you know if he and I have any other siblings?"

Dennis didn't what to tell her anything, but since there was a good chance she would learn about Maddie, he had to be truthful. "You and Ethan have two sisters," he said, keeping back an important bit of information about the two girls from her.

"Really? How exciting. I would like to meet them someday. Do you know where they live?"

Dennis had to choose his words carefully, as he didn't what her to know all of the truth just yet, as she may change her mind about helping Ethan. "Maddie lives in Montana," he said, hoping Lisa didn't ask him where Ethan lived. "Last we heard, your other sister was living in Illinois," he stated truthfully, as that had been her last known address.

"I guess that means I won't be seeing either of them anytime soon. Was Maddie tested as a donor?"

Dennis wasn't sure how to answer her question, as he felt he was sitting on a time bomb. If he told her too much information, he might accidentally give something away that could ruin everything he was trying to accomplish here.

He had to clear his throat before he gave her his answer. "She wasn't tested because she's showing signs of the disease as well. The doctors in Montana are hoping if you're a match for Ethan, then you'll be able to help Maddie as well."

She felt good, but since her siblings were sick, it only made sense she would eventually get the disease as well. "If two of my siblings have the disease, won't

I have it too?" she asked, because why would the sickness miss her.

"We won't know until you're tested." Of course, he didn't tell her, that the doctors had assured him that it was unlikely that she had it.

"Hopefully, I don't have the disease and will be a match. Can I come see Ethan?"

"Yes, of course. How soon can you be here?"

"Fifteen to twenty minutes, depending on the traffic."

"Ethan is in room 451. We'll see you when you get here."

After Lisa hung up, she put her hand on top of Grayson's and looked up at him. "I'm going to meet my brother," she said excitedly.

"You think he's really your brother?"

"I can only hope so. My mother didn't know anything about my biological family other than my mother wasn't able to raise me."

"Do you mind if I go with you?" Grayson asked as he looked deeply into her eyes, hoping she would agree to allow him to go with her.

She squeezed his hand, her heart swelling at his offer. Maybe, just maybe this meant he had feeling for her, she could only hope. "I'd like that very much."

***

When they reached Ethan's room, Grayson took hold of her hand before she could enter the room and gave it a light squeeze. "I'll be just outside," he said, though his tone was more like, *I'll be here if you should need me*.

"Grayson, I want you to meet Ethan."

"Maybe another time, right now it should just be you and him."

"Okay," she said. She leaned over and kissed his cheek, then turned and stepped into the room, leaving a stunned Grayson at the door staring after her.

As she walked into the room, her eyes went to the young man in the bed. Seeing how pale his skin color was, she realized he was very sick and made a quick prayer that she would be able to save his life. What surprised her most was that he looked to be her age, but how could that possible?

As she walked towards the bed, she studied him, trying to see if they looked alike. Seeing his brown hair and brown eyes, she frowned, as she didn't see how they could be siblings, as her hair was auburn and her eyes were green.

When she reached the bed, Lisa put her hand out to the brother and smiled at him. "I'm Lisa," she said, as her hand moved towards him.

Ethan weakly moved his hand up to meet hers. "It's nice to meet you. I don't know how to thank you for coming."

"No problem. I want to know what makes you think I'm your sister as we don't even look alike?"

With his parents standing there watching him with fear in their eyes, he had to bite his lip from telling her exactly how he was positive they were siblings. "Your adoptive parents' lawyer told my father where you worked." Ethan then introduced his parents, Delores and Dennis to Lisa, keeping a very important fact about them back from her.

When Lisa looked over at the couple, she was surprised to see how much Ethan looked like his adoptive father. A swift suspicion began creeping through her mind, one so awful she didn't like to think about, so she quickly removed it from her head.

"I'm sorry you're so sick, I just hope I can help you and Maddie get better."

"You'll have to be tested, and if we're a match and aren't sick, then we're good to go for the bone marrow transplant. I must tell you that it may take you several weeks, maybe even a few months for you to fully recuperate from the procedure."

"I did some research on the Internet regarding the procedure, so I know what to expect. I don't care about that if there's a chance I can save yours and our sister's life. If we do this; my boss says I can work from home until I'm able to return to the office to work."

"You must have a great boss."

"I do," she said, not realizing she had blushed at her comment. "But being siblings isn't there a possibility that I'm already affected?"

"Yes, there is. The doctors don't know what caused the immune disease in the first place and are hoping that since we lived in Montana and you lived here, maybe you won't be affected." As soon as he spoke the words, he cringed as the last thing his father had told him was not to let Lisa know they lived in the same state as Maddie.

Lisa was surprised to learn where he lived, but refrained commenting on it, as her thoughts were thinking her suspicion hadn't been off after all.

When Ethan saw her surprised look about where he lived, he knew she was starting to put two and two together, so he knew he had to do something about it before she could refuse to help. If he was going to live with himself, he had to do the right thing, so he looked at his parents. "I hate to ask, but I would like a few minutes alone with Lisa."

"Ethan, can't that wait until another time?" Dennis asked with a petrified look on his face.

"No, Dad it can't."

Dennis remained quiet, but gave his son a look that said *Don't say anything to mess up this opportunity.* He nodded at his son, and then he took hold of his wife's hand and they left the room.

Once the door was shut, Ethan took hold of Lisa's hand. "I have something to tell you that might change your mind about helping me?"

As Lisa stared at him, she realized she was about to learn the truth about this situation. If he told her what she thought he was going to say, she wondered if the information would change her mind about helping the brother she'd just found.

He studied her as he watched the different emotions crossed her face. "Are you ready?"

"I guess so," she replied nervously.

"Dennis and Delores are our biological parents," he said, watching her expression closely as his words soaked into her brain.

Tears began to appear in her eyes. "Didn't they want me?"

Ethan's hand reached out and grasped hers. "It wasn't like that. You see, Mom was only seventeen at the time of our birth.

"*Our* birth?" she asked her eyes wide with this new information.

"You and I are out of a set of quadruplets."

"Quadruplets?" she asked, shocked to learn this information.

"Yes, consisting of a set of triplets and one single birth, you being the single birth," he said, feeling a bit better at telling her part of what he'd held back earlier from her. "Even though you were born at the same time as the rest of us, we're hoping you won't have the disease and will be able to heal Maddie and me."

"I always felt as if part of me was missing, and now that I know I have siblings, I know why."

"How does it feel to know you're part of a set of quadruplets?"

"I'm surprised to say the least," she muttered.

Ethan gave her a weak smile. "I hope it wasn't a bad surprise."

She laughed. "No, just an unexpected one. So how come they kept you, but not the rest of us?"

Ethan's heart ached as he had more bad news to tell her. "Our mother still had a year of high school and since she didn't have any idea where our father was at the time, she put us up for adoption to give us the best life possible," he stopped unsure how to tell her the rest.

"Go on. I want to know the story."

"By the time Dad returned to town, yours, and our other sister's adoptions had already gone through. They canceled Maddie and my adoption, got married, and moved in with our mother's parents."

"So you're saying; you and Maddie grew up with our parents?" Her heart began aching as his words registered that he and one of their sisters hadn't been given away like a piece of unwanted property.

"Yes, we did."

Tears began running down Lisa's cheeks. "So when did you and Maddie learn about me?" she asked, assuming he'd say they just found out about her.

"We've always known about you as Mom has a picture of the four of us on the day we were born," he told her, keeping the rest of the story to himself.

"Do you know anything about our other sister?"

"We haven't been able to locate her as of yet. Her adoptive parents had been keeping Mom informed about her life over the years, but then the letters stopped coming, and we assumed her parents had died. Since she didn't know she was adopted or anything about any of us, she never knew to contact us."

"I see." His statement brought a pain to her chest. If they knew where their other sister had been living, did that mean they also knew where she was all this time?

"Do you want to think about this before you commit yourself to the procedure?"

She was fighting to prevent the tears. "I have one more question," she stated with a crack in her voice.

"Okay, what is it?" he asked, knowing she was trying not to cry in front of him.

"How long have they known where I lived?" she asked, prepared for the worst.

Ethan looked down at his hands. This was the information he had kept from her earlier, as he was hoping she wouldn't ever have to find out about this. "Always," he replied softly.

"Always?" she sobbed, as she really didn't want to believe this was true.

"Your adoptive parents kept in contact with Mom, sending pictures of you in letters over the years."

"Did my parents know I had three siblings?" she asked, almost afraid to hear his answer.

"No, they never knew about the rest of us."

"Why not?" she demanded.

Ethan looked embarrassed, and had to clear his throat before he could continue. "Mom didn't want anyone to know she was selling us separately so she could receive more money."

With tears filling her eyes, she stood, her eyes never leaving his. "I'll be tested, and if I'm a match, I'll donate whatever is necessary for you and Maddie. I won't mind seeing you again and Maddie when she's better, but I don't want to ever see your parents again."

Ethan's heart broke at her words. "Lisa, they're your parents too."

"No, my parents were James and Paula Tidwell." She then turned and walked out the door. Without looking look over at her biological parent, she walked to Grayson, took hold of his hand, and started them for the elevator.

Grayson seeing she was upset, didn't question why she hadn't said anything to Ethan's parents, so they waited for the elevator in silence.

When the door opened, she pulled him inside with her, and keeping her eyes down, she waited for the doors to close. And soon as the doors were completely closed, Lisa turned and threw herself into Grayson's arms and began sobbing.

It took a while before he learned the whole story of why she was so upset and had refused to speak to either of the VanCamps. Tearfully, she told him about being part of a set of quadruplets, the other two were sisters; one grew up in Montana with Ethan and their biological parents, while the other sister lived in Illinois.

Being shocked by her story was an understatement.

***

When Lisa stormed out of their son's room, and then hurried straight towards her friend without once looking over at them, Dennis and Delores realized something was most definitely wrong. Afraid Ethan had told her too much, the two rushed into Ethan's room.

"Is she going to do it?" Delores asked her son, hoping he hadn't told Lisa something that had changed her change her mind about helping her brother.

"She'll be tested, and if she isn't sick and is a match, she'll donate her bone marrow for Maddie and me."

"I hear a *but* here," Dennis said.

"She doesn't want anything to do with the two of you," he stated, not even trying to soften his words.

"But we're her parents," Delores sobbed.

"Mom, you gave up that right the day you sold her."

"You told her that I sold her?" she yelled at her son.

Ethan looked at his mother with cold eyes. "Did you or did you not receive money for my sisters when they were adopted?"

"What was I supposed to do? I had to support myself."

"Maddie and I were lucky as we had each other, but our sisters hadn't any idea they had siblings out there in the world."

"They had two parents that loved them, and they grew up in good homes," Delores said in her defense.

"Yes they did, but now those loving parents are gone from their lives, and they're all alone."

Delores' eyes filled with anger. "And you think that's my fault."

"No, but when you assumed their parents had passed away, you could have contacted them and introduced yourself, tell them they had family that wanted to meet them."

Delores shook her head. "What if they didn't know they were adopted? I was afraid that if I contacted them and told them I was their biological mother, and they hadn't known, it could cause unnecessary pain for them."

"Well, all that doesn't matter now, as that's exactly what Lisa is going through now."

***

Lisa was tested to see if she had the disease, and when she got the test results back, she cried. Not only didn't she have any signs of the immune disease, the doctors didn't think she would ever contact the deadly ailment, as her chemical makeup was different from her siblings.

When the DNA results came back, it showed Lisa was a match. Not wanting to run into Ethan's parents, as she refused to think of them as hers, Lisa called her brother and told him that she would be donating her bone marrow for him and their sister. Ethan was thrill with her news, and thanked her several times, for what she was doing to them.

CHAPTER EIGHTEEN

Since Lisa was having her bone marrow harvested tomorrow morning, she and Grayson were busy getting manuscripts ready so she would have plenty of work while she was at home recuperating. Concentrating with what she was doing, she didn't realize that it was lunchtime and that they were the only ones in office.

When her tummy growled, she looked at the clock and was surprised to see the time. She left her desk and hurried to the kitchen to grab her lunch sack. Just as in her dream, Lisa was returning to her desk and just as she turned the last corner, she ran smack into Chuck O'Bannon's chest, the same as she had in her nightmare.

When she looked up at the man's face and saw who it was, she let out a scream as she knew from her dream that Grayson was already dead and Chuck was about to strangle her to death.

When Grayson heard Lisa scream, he ran out his office door, only to run smack into Chuck's back. "What's going on here?"

Chuck hunched his shoulders, as if to say 'I don't know'. "All I know is that as soon as she saw me, she started screaming," he said, stunned by the petrified look on the young woman's face.

"Where's your gun?" she boldly asked him.

"Gun?" Chuck was shocked by her question. "Why would I have a gun?"

"Aren't you here to kill Grayson?" she asked bravely.

Chuck's eyes grew wide. "Where did you get a crazy idea like that?"

"Do you deny that you threatened to kill Grayson because he wasn't supporting your niece?"

He cringed at her statement. "I'm sorry about that. I shouldn't have said that, but I was angry, and it sort of just popped out of my mouth. I don't have a gun, and I'm not here to kill anyone."

Hearing that, Lisa let out a deep sigh.

"So what are you doing here Chuck?" Grayson asked the man.

"It's important that I talk to you," Chuck insisted.

"Can't this wait until later? We're short on time here, so I don't have any time to spare."

"No it can't wait, I have a babysitter for Anne, but I need to get back to her."

Chuck's statement confused him. "Where's Sharron?"

"That's why I'm here."

"Okay, I'll give you ten minutes," he said, remaining where he was.

"Here?" he asked as he looked over at Lisa.

"Why not?"

"Fine," he uttered in a disgusted voice. "I want a written statement that you give up all your legal rights to Anne."

Grayson shook his head at Chuck's words.

"You're refusing to give me one," he demanded loudly, as he thought Grayson would jump at the chance of sign over his rights to the child he didn't want.

"No, that isn't what I meant. You don't need me to sign a release, as Anne isn't my child."

"What? Of course she is," Chuck stated. "Sharron was your wife."

"I was hoping Sharron would have told you by now. Since she hasn't, you should know that she had an affair with Dale, the ex-boyfriend, while we were married. He's the father of Anne, so he's the one you need to be talking to."

"Do you know where I can find him?"

"Sorry, can't help you there as the last I'd heard was he wasn't even living in town."

"Then I guess this matter doesn't concern you." Chuck discouraged by the recent news, turned, and started for the door, worried what to do about Anne.

"Chuck, what matter are you referring to?"

He always liked Grayson and needing to talk to someone, he turned back around.

Seeing the man's tears, Grayson became concerned. "Talk to me Chuck, tell me what's going on and maybe I can help."

"Sharron's in the hospital as she collapsed last night. She's very sick and isn't expected to live much longer than a few more months. Since Anne deserves two parents raising her, I've decided that after my sister dies, I'm putting the baby up for adoption."

Grayson was stunned by the first part of his statement. "What's wrong with Sharron?"

Chuck shook his head. "The doctor says it's some form of a rare immune system disease I've never heard of before."

"What are they doing to help her?"

"They say there isn't much hope for her as the survival rate is nonexistent without a bone marrow transplant. They're trying to find a match for her, but they haven't had any luck so far. What's strange is that there are two other cases at that same hospital, but it looks hopeful for them, as a sibling is donating their marrow for them."

Grayson gave Chuck a puzzled look at the thought of three people having a rare immune system disease at the same hospital. "Have you been tested to see if you can donate bone marrow for her?"

Chuck just shook his head. "There isn't a need, Sharron was adopted, and the baby is too young to be a donor."

Grayson hadn't made a connection between Sharron and Ethan's illness until he heard his ex-wife had been adopted. "Sharron never mentioned to me that she was adopted."

"That's because she doesn't know. I was five when she came to us, so I knew, but my parents never told her. Over the years, I simply forgot that fact, as to me, she was simply my baby sister."

Grayson looked over at Lisa, wondering if Sharron could be Lisa's remaining sister, as he knew Chuck and Sharron had lived in Illinois until the death of their parents.

"Lisa, did Ethan mention anything about fourth sibling, other than she lived in Illinois?"

"Only that she didn't know she had been adopted as a baby."

"What are you two talking about?" Chuck asked as he looked back and forth between the two.

"Lisa was adopted as a baby and has just found out she has a brother and sister who are sick with what sounds like the same disease as Sharron has." Suddenly a thought came to him that might help decide if Sharron could be Lisa's other sister. "Lisa, when is your birthday?"

Lisa gasped. "You think your ex-wife is my sister?"

"Maybe," he said, as he could be way off base on his assumption.

"Sister?" Chuck looked at Lisa, then over at Grayson. "What are you two talking about?"

"Let Lisa answer and then I'll tell you."

"August fifteenth. What's Sharron's?"

Grayson clapped his hands together. "What a coincidence, Sharron has the same birthday as you do, so it's possible that she's the fourth sibling."

Then he shook his head, as Lisa had red hair and Sharron had brown hair, not only that, but the two didn't look anything alike. But since he hadn't seen Ethan at the hospital, maybe Sharron took after him. That is if she was indeed part of Lisa's family.

"Chuck, do you have a picture of Sharron with you?"

"Yes, I have one of her with Anne just after she was born."

"Could we see it please?"

Chuck pulled out his billfold, opened it, and flipped it to the picture. Part of him hoped that once Grayson saw her picture, he would claim the child as his, while the other part knew he had told the truth about Dale being Anne's father.

"Lisa, I want you to look at Sharron and tell me if she looks anything like Maddie and Ethan."

Lisa looked down at the picture and gasped.

"What is it?" Grayson asked softly. "Does she look like either of them?"

She nodded her head as tears ran down her cheeks. "You're right; your ex-wife is my other sister, as she's the splitting image of Maddie."

"Damn!" he replied, figuring Lisa wouldn't want anything to do with him now that she knew he was her sister's ex-husband.

Lisa gave him a puzzled look at his swearing. "What's wrong now?"

He shook his head, as he couldn't very well tell her what he'd been thinking. "This is such a bizarre twist of fate." He turned and looked over at Chuck. "Lisa has been tested and is a perfect bone marrow match for her brother and other sister. Since Sharron is the third triplet, then Lisa will be a match for her as well. The procedure is taking place the first thing tomorrow morning for her other two siblings, so they could simply add Sharron to the procedure."

As tears ran down his cheeks, Chuck grabbed Lisa and hugged her to him. "I don't know how I'll ever be able to thank you for donating your bone marrow. Will you go out to dinner with me sometime so I can thank you?" he asked with a hopefully look.

Lisa was surprised by his actions and his invitation. "You're welcome, but we don't know yet if I'll be able to save Ethan and Maddie, let alone Sharron." She thought about refusing his dinner request, but if Grayson wasn't interested having a relationship with her, maybe Chuck would be. "I'd be happy to have dinner with you, but first let see if I can help Sharron as we don't know if they can take enough marrow for three people."

Grayson was stunned by what he'd just witnessed. Hearing her accept the date from Chuck, he knew that if he didn't let Lisa know how he felt about her right away, she would soon be someone else's girl. But for now, his declaration had to wait.

"I think we should go to the hospital and tell Sharron about all this," Grayson told them.

"Let me get Anne and I'll meet you in the hospital in the front lobby."

* * *

When they arrived, Chuck was waiting for them with the baby sleeping in his arms. Lisa was touched how lovingly her uncle held her and knew he would hate putting the baby up for adoption if things didn't end well for his sister.

As they rode up in the elevator, Grayson told Chuck that he should be the one to tell his sister about being adopted. Chuck nervous of how she was going to take the news, disagreed, and said Lisa should be the one to tell her about their relationship since she was her biological sister and was donating her bone marrow to save her life

Grayson disagreed, saying Sharon didn't know Lisa, and besides he thought it would be easier on Sharron if she received the news from her brother.

As the threesome stepped into the room, Lisa's eyes went directly to her sister and gasped at how bad Sharron looked. Sharron wasn't as ill as Ethan and Maddie, who she'd met last night, but Sharron would be if she didn't get help soon.

Grayson took hold of her hand as they continued to the bed.

Sharron was surprised to see the group with Chuck, especially Anne. With her daughter being here, she took it as a sign that this would be the last time she'd ever see her baby. She was angry that Grayson was here with his girlfriend, figuring he was here to rub her affair in her face, telling her she was getting what she deserved.

The group moved closer to her bed, once there, Chuck laid his niece in Sharron's arms. He sat down on the side of the bed and took hold of her hand.

She looked over at her brother, confused by his petrified look. "If you have bad news, just spit it out and get it over with."

"I have bad news and good news," Chuck said slowly, as his mind tried to find the words to tell her why they were all here.

When Chuck looked over at Lisa, she could tell he was having a rough time spitting out the words he needed to say. Seeing his scared expression, she knew she had to be the one to tell Sharron the news. "Let me tell her," she said, as she sat down on the other side of the bed. "First of all, I'd like to introduce myself," Lisa said as she smiled at Sharron.

"You're Grayson new girlfriend," Sharron stated coldly.

Lisa blushed as she wished it was true. "No, I'm Lisa Tidwell, I work for Grayson."

"I'm sorry if I sounded rude," Sharron said. "It's my fault my marriage is over, not yours."

"That's okay. I want to tell you that the day after you were born, you were adopted by Jeff and Lena O'Bannon."

Sharron looked over at Chuck. "Is this true?"

"Yes."

"How long have you known?" she asked tearfully.

"All my life," he replied honestly. "But that has never mattered, as I have always loved you as my sister."

Sharron smiled. "Yes, you have." She turned back to Lisa. "What's the good news?"

Lisa then proceeded to tell Sharron that they were sisters, and she was going to donate her bone marrow in order to try and save her life. She continued with her story, explaining how their mother had put the two of them up for adoption, leaving out the part about being sold to their adoptive parents.

She divulged that they were part of a set of quadruplets and that Sharron, a brother, and a sister were triplets, while she had been the odd man out. She continued with her story about Ethan and Maddie being sick and that she was to donating her bone marrow to them as well.

Throughout the whole story telling, Sharron just listened as tears ran down her face. She was speechless to learn Lisa was going to save her life. She was now hopeful that maybe her child wasn't going to grow up without a mother; she smiled and thanked God for this miracle.

When her story was over, Lisa turned to look at Chuck. "How was that?"

"Better than I could have done." He turned back to Sharron. "The bone marrow transplant is scheduled for the first thing tomorrow morning. It may take a while before we know if it's going to work, but at least now you have a chance of recovery."

"While we are all here together," Grayson started, "I want you to tell Chuck who the father of your daughter is."

Sharron looked over at her brother, ashamed of her behavior regarding her adultery, her eyes dropped to her hand. "Grayson isn't the father, and I have DNA proof of that fact."

Chuck turned to Grayson. "I'm sorry for the way I've acted. Will you accept my apology?"

"Yes, I will. And let's pledge never to speak of this ever again." Grayson then put his hand out to his ex-brother-in-law, who may still be part of his life since Sharron turned out to be Lisa's sister.

"I agree," Chuck said, and then reached over to shake Grayson's hand.

EPILOGUE

The next morning, as the group waited for their loved ones to come through the surgery, Grayson introduce Chuck to Dennis and Delores as their other daughter's brother.

Dennis said they wanted to meet Sharron, but all Chuck could say was that as of last night, Sharron wasn't ready to meet them just yet. But she did want to meet Maddie and Ethan.

Everything regarding the procedure had gone off well, but it was still too soon to know if it was successful. The three patients would remain in the hospital until it was known one way or the other, but Lisa had been released to go home.

She had just finished packing her suitcase when she heard someone entering her room. "I'm ready to go," she said, thinking Chuck had arrived to take her home. When she turned, she was surprised to see Grayson standing there.

"Grayson, what are you doing here?" she asked.

"I'm here to take you home."

"You didn't have to do that. Chuck was going to drive me home."

Grayson sat down on her bed and took hold of her hand, pulling her down beside him. "I don't want you to go out to dinner with Chuck."

Lisa laughed. "He wasn't asking me for a date, simply wanted to thank me for helping Sharron."

"I say you're wrong," he insisted.

She was confused by his reply. "Why does it matter to you one way or the other?"

"This isn't how or where I wanted to tell you this."

"Tell me what?" she asked shakily, for in her mind, she figured he was going to fire her because she was his ex-wife's sister.

Grayson squeezed her hand as he looked deeply into her eyes. "I'm in love with you."

"You are?" she asked tearfully.

"Yes, and that's why I don't want you to go out with Chuck."

"I'm not interested in Chuck that way, and I don't think he's interested in me."

"Of course he is. You're a beautiful woman who has saved his sister's life."

"When I go out with him, I'll make sure he knows that I'm not interested in a relationship with him."

***

The entire group waited impatiently for any sign that the transplant had worked for the three sick siblings. The first few hours slowly passed without any of them showing any improvement, and the only thing that kept their hopes up was that none of them had gotten any worse. Still unsure if the procedure had been a success, emotions were high one moment, and down the next. It was the hardest on Dennis and Delores, as only the two children they'd raise would speak to them.

Chuck brought Anne to the hospital often to see her mother, but Sharron was too weak to do more than just hold her. In her mind, she was saying good-bye to her daughter, and had already written up a legal document giving Chuck custody of Anne.

It was on the third day that the test results finally showed signs of improvement. The doctors told them this was a good outcome, but the family was still afraid to get their hopes up. By the time the tenth day arrived, Sharron and Maddie were able to leave the hospital, and by the fifteenth day, Ethan was ready to go home to Montana.

On the day of his release, the four congregated in Ethan's room to get acquainted with their siblings, and they formed a bond, which was surprising since only Ethan and Maddie had always known the other. There was a lot of laughter, but the fun came to an abrupt end when Dennis and Delores stepped into the room.

"Lisa and Sharron, your father and I are sorry how things turned out regarding your adoptions. Ethan said I should have found a way to keep you both, but since I didn't, all I can say is that I'm sorry. I probably could have put an end to each of your adoptions, but your parents were so thrilled in having you as their daughters that I didn't have the heart to tell them I wanted you back."

Lisa took pity on her biological mother. "Delores, I can only imagine how hard it was on you to make the decision to give up your four babies. I'm sorry how I acted when I found out the truth, but I was in shock at learning you'd given two of us away. I have to thank you for not ending the pregnancy, as then none of us would be here today. I think we should forget the past and start over." She looked over at Sharron. "Do you think you can forgive our mother?"

Sharron nodded. "We all make mistakes, me included, so I'm all for starting over."

There were a lot of hugging and tears as the two sisters accepted their biological parents into their lives.

***

When Chuck called Lisa to set up a time for their dinner, she told him that she was interested in Grayson, so she couldn't go out with him. Chuck assured her that this wasn't a date, simply a dinner thanking her for saving his sister's life. He wished her luck with Grayson, saying he thought he was a good man.

She did go out to dinner with Chuck and it was a strange meal, as Grayson, Sharron, and the baby went with them. The two ex-spouses were uncomfortable being together, but neither of them said anything derogatory to the other.

As Sharron watched her ex-husband, she quickly realized that the reason Grayson was with them for this meal was because he was interested in Lisa. The feeling was a bit disheartening to her at knowing Grayson wanted her sister, but then it was her fault her marriage had ended and no one else's.

***

When Grayson and Lisa started dating, they tried to keep their relationship a secret from the others in the office. When Grayson didn't think he could hide his feelings for her any longer, he proposed marriage and Lisa tearfully accepted.

Of course, the first thing Lisa worried about was how Sharron would take the news that she was going to marry her ex-husband. Since she couldn't very well keep it a secret, she went over to Chuck's home to tell Sharron that she was going to marry Grayson.

Sharron told her that she was happy for her sister, and the two spent time together preparing for her wedding, but the one thing they never talked about was their relationship with Grayson as that was taboo.

On the day of their wedding the church was full of their family and friends, and luckily it went off without a hitch.

***

Dale wanting to spend time with his daughter started visiting Anne at her mother's home, as he didn't feel comfortable handling his newborn daughter on his own yet. The more Dale saw Sharron, the more he realized he still have feelings for her, and when Anne was three months old, Dale and Sharron were married.

It was at Sharron's wedding reception that Lisa announced to their family and friends that she and Grayson were going to have a baby in seven months and the family was thrilled. Jayna and Christa not wanting to take away from Lisa's announcement remained quiet about their second pregnancy as there was plenty of time as they too, were expecting in seven months.

CPSIA information can be obtained
at www.ICGtesting.com
Printed in the USA
LVHW020009280423
745413LV00009B/174

9 781960 629494